WESTERN WP PROMISES

Texas Trouble

KATHLEEN O'BRIEN

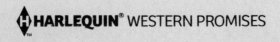

Recycling programs
for this product may
not exist in your area.

ISBN-13: 978-0-373-00370-9

Texas Trouble

Printed in U.S.A.

www.Harlequin.com

Kathleen O'Brien was a feature writer and TV critic before marrying a fellow journalist. Motherhood, which followed soon after, was so marvelous she turned to writing novels, which meant she could work at home. Though she's a lifelong city gal, she has a special place in her heart for tiny towns like Silverdell, where you may not enjoy a lot of privacy…but you never really face your troubles alone, either.

Books by Kathleen O'Brien

Harlequin Superromance

Visit the Author Profile page at Harlequin.com for more titles.

To my much-loved mother and daughter,
who shared that extraordinary day with me.
I wish we could do it again.

And to the Audubon Center for Birds of Prey,
for working magic year after year.

Chapter One

A dragonfly hovered inches from Nora Archer's shoulder, its wings hypnotically beating the warm air of the hacienda courtyard. She ought to get up, get going, get Sean ready for Little League, but peaceful moments were too rare these days. She used to love sitting out here in the late afternoon, when the Bull's Eye Ranch was quiet, the shadows stretched across the bricks, and the breeze was full of honeysuckle and wind chimes.

Milly, the housekeeper, was vacuuming on the second floor, a way of keeping an eye on Sean without making him feel like a prisoner. So, temporarily off duty, Nora lay on the lounger, prepared to steal a few more minutes.

A battle was coming with Sean, and she wasn't eager to engage. They'd quarreled as soon as he got home from school, about whether his homework could wait until after the game. She hadn't budged, though as always she'd needed to steel herself against the pain behind his angry hazel eyes. He was only nine… He'd been through so much….

But dealing with Sean called for discipline and routine, not sloppy emotion and inconsistency. So she'd held firm. As usual, he'd stomped upstairs in a fury and slammed his door.

Most days, after a scene like that, she would send Harry up to remind Sean it was time to shower and put on his uniform. No matter how prickly Sean was with his mother, no matter how sour he'd grown about his former love, baseball, he never took it out on Harry.

The hero-worship of a little brother had once been the bane of Sean's existence, but not anymore. These days, Harry was the only one Sean seemed to trust.

Unfortunately, Harry was playing at a friend's house.

So for just a few minutes more, she wanted

to watch the dragonfly, bask in the spring sunshine, and pretend everything was normal. She wanted to pretend that her boys had a father, who at any moment might come whistling around the corner, shouldering a trio of fishing poles. She wanted to pretend that Sean hadn't grown surly and difficult, that he hadn't begun to hate everything he used to love, and that his nights were peaceful under acres of starry Archer sky, not haunted by nightmares of madmen, guns and fear.

A lovely fantasy, but it couldn't last. Too soon the quiet hour was gone. She opened her eyes and saw that the sunlight had abandoned the last inch of courtyard, the shadow of the tiled roofline on the west touching the shadow of the tupelo on the east.

She sat up. Had she just heard a sound... maybe a car coming through the iron gates at the front of the hacienda?

Evelyn, already? Could it really be almost five?

Nora's sister-in-law had agreed to picked up Harry and meet them here so that they could ride to the game together. Darn. Nora had hoped to get the war with Sean over and won before Evelyn showed up to witness it.

Evelyn always meant well, but the older

woman always preferred sandpaper to honey, so she and Nora rarely agreed about how to handle even the smallest parenting issues.

Nora was tugging on her sneakers when, suddenly, the air seemed to burst into chaotic sound.

First, the shrill ringing of the telephone. She felt around under the lounger for the cordless handset. Just as her fingers closed around it, a whoosh of air swept through the courtyard, followed by the bang of the massive wood-and-iron front door.

Then voices. Her sister-in-law's agitated alto. "Sean Archer! I told you I want an answer! What have you been doing?"

"Sean!" The short, high-pitched squeal of the housekeeper, Milly. "How did you get out? What happened to you?"

And, finally, the tearful defiance of her older son. "I didn't do it. I don't care what they say. I didn't do it."

Nora flew into the great room, the telephone still ringing in her hand. She determined first that Sean was all in one piece—and so was Harry, who stood holding Evelyn's hand, eyes wide. Clearly upset, all of them, but no one seriously hurt.

Then she noticed that Sean was covered in dirt, and his left cheek was bleeding.

"I found him trying to sneak in through the side loggia. Look at him! God only knows what he's been up to." Evelyn tried to grab Sean's shirt, but he ducked away. "Explain yourself, Sean!"

Nora winced at the tone, which was guaranteed to make Sean—or anyone—mulish. "Honey," she said more gently. "What happened?"

He took one step toward his mother, as though his instinct was to run to her arms. But then he checked himself. His eyebrows drew together, and his jaw jutted out. "I didn't do it. That guy is a liar."

Harry had no scruples about racing over and burrowing his face into his mother's stomach. "Sean's bleeding, Mom. His face is bleeding."

"I see that. But it doesn't look too bad, really." Nora kept her hand on Harry's carroty curls, but she focused her gaze on her older son. She fought to keep her voice calm. "What guy, Sean?"

"Over at Two Wings. That son of a—"

Evelyn, whose weather-beaten face was every bit as grim as her nephew's, raised her palm. "Sean Archer. We don't use words like that."

Nora felt a twinge of frustration. Bad language obviously wasn't the real problem here. Two Wings, a newly constructed private bird sanctuary, was the property next door to Bull's Eye Ranch. But in Texas terms, *next door* meant maybe a mile away. Could Sean possibly have been at Two Wings while she thought he was safely pouting in his room?

Without meeting Evelyn's reproachful eyes, she bent down and spoke steadily to her son. "What guy at Two Wings? Do you mean Mr. Cathcart?"

"No." He wiped at his cheek, his fist coming away streaked with dark red mud. Nora saw gratefully that the skin beneath was no longer bleeding—a fairly superficial scrape. "I mean Mr. Cathcart's manager. He's probably the one who was calling just now."

Nora glanced down at the phone in her hand. It had given up its demands and gone silent, cycling over to voice mail.

Sean sniffed. "He thinks I killed a bird. But I didn't."

"Killed?" Evelyn's voice roared. "For God's sake, Sean, what did you—"

"I told you I *didn't,*" Sean began hotly.

"Evelyn, please—"

"Mom," Harry broke in, his voice rising as he absorbed the agitation around him. "Mom, is Sean okay? Does he have to go to the hospital?" The little boy's voice trembled, and his arms tightened around her waist. "We don't like the hospital."

Her heart squeezed hard at the childish understatement, and all the pain that lay behind it. Little boys shouldn't have the kinds of memories her sons had. They should barely know what hospitals were for.

"Of course not," she said with authority. "It's just a tiny scrape."

Harry lifted his face, brightening, but Sean's expression grew darker. His hazel eyes flashed, and his red eyebrows dug down toward the bridge of his nose. "I still want to go to the game."

"You must be joking," Evelyn snapped. "Do you think this kind of behavior will be rewarded by—"

"It's not a reward!" Sean interrupted his aunt without thinking, but Nora cringed inside, well aware that the older woman had already been offended, and would now be doubly so. Every social faux pas the boys committed was proof, in Evelyn's eyes, that Nora hadn't taught them manners...or respect for their aunt.

"I hate baseball." Sean turned to Nora. "But you said it was a commitment, remember? You said when people made commitments they had to follow through, and—"

"This is different."

Nora knew what she'd said, but she also knew the rules about being consistent with your parenting message. Whoever invented those rules must never have been a parent.

"We need to get that cheek looked at. And then you've got a lot of explaining to do. Most importantly, if you've been in some kind of trouble over at Two Wings, we need to talk to Mr. Cathcart."

"We certainly do," Evelyn agreed.

"No!" Sean wheeled on her, his hands fisted. "Not you! Why would *you* go?"

Oh, God, could this get any worse? Nora tossed her sister-in-law a smile, asking her to understand that Sean was afraid, and undoubtedly ashamed. He loved his aunt. He probably just didn't want any extra witnesses to his disgrace.

But Evelyn didn't understand. Nora could see by the narrowing of her eyes. She looked as if she'd been struck. Evelyn Archer Gellner was a tough Texas widow, pure steel from the inside out. But the boys, her only blood relations left in this world, were her Achilles' heel. They could break her heart by simply twitching away from her kiss.

If only she could lose some of that barking bossiness, perhaps they could enjoy her more. But right now Evelyn's wounded pride was not the focus.

"I want you to go upstairs with Milly," Nora said quietly. "I want you to wash up and change into clean clothes. I'm going to call Mr. Cathcart."

"He's going to be mad. Because his manager is a liar, and—"

"Sean. Enough."

Sean recognized his mother's tone, and he took in a huge breath, preparing to throw a fit. But Milly, who had worked at the ranch since Nora's late husband had been a little boy— and, thus, for the duration of their marriage— recognized the tone, too. This discussion was over. She swooped in and took Sean by the arm before he could get out the first furious syllable.

"Come on," Milly said. Sean balked, digging in his heels, but Milly, who could see three hundred from her spot on the scales, just grinned. "You don't want me to have to sling you over my shoulder like a sack of potatoes, now, do you? With your little brother looking on?"

At that threat, Harry mustered the courage to leave his spot in Nora's embrace. He walked over to his big brother and took his hand.

"I know you didn't kill anything, Sean," he said. "Really. And Mom knows, too."

Born to be a peacemaker, Nora thought with a rush of tenderness. And thank God they had one in the family these days. Evelyn looked like a thundercloud, and Sean's scowl was almost as fierce.

But then Sean glanced toward Nora, and for a minute she thought she saw something else hiding behind the hostility. Something like... *hope.*

Hope that she believed in him.

In spite of the other sins, the tempers, the sneaking out, the running away and whatever had caused all that mud and blood, he wanted her to trust that he hadn't done anything as terrible as destroy a living creature.

"Harry's right," she said, praying it was true. "I know you didn't kill anything." She ignored the intake of breath from Evelyn, who clearly thought she was, once again, being too soft.

Refusing to meet her sister-in-law's outraged gaze, Nora watched as Milly and the boys climbed the winding staircase, Sean dragging his dirty hand along the iron railing. When they rounded the first curve, she called up the voice mail.

"Nora," an elegant baritone said smoothly, "this is Logan Cathcart. My manager just said your son was at the sanctuary. He was— He'd been—" A short silence. "It's nothing serious, but… I think we should talk."

She shook her head, frustrated, and clicked the button. "He didn't leave any details," she said, for Evelyn's benefit.

She began scrolling through the handset's electronic address book. "I'd better call him and see what really happened. His message said it wasn't serious, but of course he might be trying not to upset me. He's a very nice man, actually."

She had just found the Two Wings's main number when she sensed Evelyn's gaze boring into the top of her head. She glanced up. Her sister-in-law's expression was even more unpleasant than Nora had imagined. It tried unsuccessfully to disguise her real anger as amusement.

"I know you want to come with us, Evvie,"

Nora said, trying to smile. "But I honestly think we'd do better alone. Sean's pride is one of his problems, and if you see him—"

"Oh, I know you would rather go alone. That doesn't surprise me. I was just surprised that… You have his number on speed dial?"

"What?" Nora looked at the handset, confused. "Whose?"

"His." Evelyn jerked her head toward the phone, as if there were someone in it. "Logan Cathcart's."

Nora's hands stilled on the keypad. She was so shocked, she couldn't think of a single response. Evelyn's face…her tone…

What could she possibly be hinting at?

But then Nora realized her silence sounded guilty. It even *felt* guilty, which was ridiculous. She had nothing to be guilty about. She hadn't spoken to Logan Cathcart, except to say hello if they passed in town, since Harrison's funeral six months ago.

She'd hardly exchanged ten words with him even then. Or for several months before Harrison's death, for that matter. Occasionally, in the middle of the night, Nora might wrestle with a guilty conscience about the handsome New Englander who had shocked Texas society by turning good cattle acres into a bird sanctuary, but Evelyn couldn't possibly know that.

Could she?

"Of course I have the Two Wings's number programmed. Why wouldn't I? They're our closest neighbors."

Evelyn's smile was cold. "And he is, as you say, such a *very* nice man. The kind of man you'd like to see…alone."

Nora set down the phone carefully on the end table beside Harrison's favorite leather couch. She faced Evelyn squarely, and waited for her to explain.

Clearly in no hurry to do so, Evelyn stared back, folding her arms neatly in front of her chest. Though she was almost sixty now, her skin leathered by years of too much sun, she was still a handsome woman. She wore her salt-and-pepper hair cut short and straight around her ears, accenting her black, bright eyes. Her body had been kept young by constant motion.

If she'd ever given a human being the same warmth she bestowed on her Jack Russell terriers, she might have been quite beautiful. In the ten years Nora had known her, though, she hadn't seen that happen.

"I'm not sure what you're trying to imply, Evelyn."

"Of course you are."

Nora hesitated, feeling as if she'd been caught on a dangerous square of an invisible chessboard. She knew that Evelyn didn't like her. For so many reasons—many of them completely justified.

From the outset, Evelyn had been suspicious of a young nobody's motives in marrying a very rich man twice her age. When it was clear she couldn't prevent the marriage, Evelyn had tried to train Nora to deserve the name Archer, but in spite of her best efforts Nora's social skills were slack, her ranching inferior.

She didn't keep the correct distance with the servants, she couldn't manage the appropriate intimacy with the horses and she never made friends easily with Harrison's business pals.

And, of course, there was the matter of Bull's Eye, the ten-thousand-acre horse and cattle ranch that had been the Archer home for generations.

Harrison had left Bull's Eye to Nora, who didn't appreciate it, involve herself in it or deserve it. Evelyn had been seething about it ever since the will was read.

Over the six months since Harrison's death,

the relationship had gone from marginal to messy. Somehow, they'd found a sliver of common ground in their mutual love for Sean and Harry, and Nora had tried to build on that.

Obviously it wasn't working today.

"Isn't that right, Nora?" Evelyn's piercing gaze hadn't flickered once. "You're secretly glad to have an excuse to call Mr. Cathcart, aren't you?"

Nora took a breath and squared her shoulders. "Evelyn, please. I don't need anything else to worry about right now. If you have something to say, say it."

"I did. I said that you have an interest in Logan Cathcart. And I'll say more. I'll say that you've been interested in him since long before your husband died."

"That's ridiculous. Where on earth did you get such an absurd idea?"

"From my brother."

Nora felt her head recoil slightly, as if she'd been slapped. "That can't be true," she said. "Harrison would never have said…"

But she couldn't finish the sentence. Harrison could have said exactly that. He *had* said it once, to Nora.

Evelyn saw Nora's dismay, and she blinked

slowly, a movement that was pained and triumphant at the same time.

"Yes, that's right. He told me. He was my brother, and he confided in me. Did you think he wouldn't? Did you think he'd suffer in silence?"

Nora shook her head. "It's just that… I hoped he would have realized how wrong he was."

"Wrong?"

"Yes. Not that I owe this explanation to you, Evvie, but he was wrong." Nora's throat felt dry. She was telling the truth, but she knew it sounded like a lie. That made her angry, almost as angry as Evelyn's constant criticism and her heavy-handed interference in the boys' lives did.

"Harrison did once suspect that I might be attracted to Logan. But I assured him it wasn't true, and he believed me. There has never been anything between Logan Cathcart and me."

She clicked Talk, and the dial tone hummed. She had a choice between two pre-programmed buttons, the Two Wings manager's office, and Logan Cathcart's home number. As her finger punched the home number defiantly, she looked up at her sister-in-law.

"And that's the last time I'll ever discuss this

with you, Evelyn, because frankly it's none of your business."

The phone began to ring. She looked toward the fireplace, signaling the end of the argument.

But she should have known she wouldn't get the last word.

"My brother has always been my business," Evelyn said quietly, her voice a deadly monotone. "And so are my brother's sons."

Nora's shoulder blades tingled, but she didn't turn around. The phone kept ringing hollowly, and she imagined it echoing through Logan Cathcart's small log-and-stone ranch house, which he'd inherited from his great-aunt.

She knew, somehow, that he was no longer there.

Illogically, the unanswered rings made her feel even more alone.

Alone with a troubled son, a haunted heart and a woman who hated her.

"I am always watching, Nora," Evelyn's voice came at her in low, hard waves. "I would never have let you hurt Harrison, and the same goes for Sean and Harry. There's nothing I won't do to protect my own flesh and blood. So be forewarned."

Chapter Two

Even before Sean Archer's unexpected visit, and the mess that followed, Logan Cathcart had been up to his eyeballs in alligators. Two candidates had shown up for the clinic tech job, but neither had any experience, so he was still administering antibiotics and changing bandages himself.

Three injured baby owls had been left in a shoebox on his doorstep overnight, and two of them didn't have a chance in hell.

Finally, the county had sent over a ream of red tape so convoluted it made his law school years look easy. He wanted to shred it up for nesting material, but since the Two Wings tax break depended on it he had to resist.

So, frankly, he hadn't been in the mood to hear that a troubled kid from the ranch next door had appeared with a dead bird in his backpack and for no apparent reason started tearing up the enclosures they'd just built yesterday.

He knew the kid's dad had died, and the family was going through a bad patch. He even felt sorry for him. His manager didn't believe the kid's story—that he'd been bringing the bird here for tending, but it died along the way—but Logan did. Somehow he just didn't think Sean Archer was that kind of crazy.

Still. A nine-year-old kid reacts to a bird's death by ripping apart everything he can reach? That didn't smell like fresh-baked mental health to Logan.

So now not only was he having to repair the damage himself, but also he was going to have to talk to Sean's mother, and that was something he'd vowed to do as little of as possible. He'd decided to steer clear of Nora Archer about two days after moving to Texas, about two minutes after meeting her.

He tossed his hammer onto the pile of wood chips and pulled the measuring tape out. He might have to order new wood. The kid must know karate—he'd really smashed things up.

"Boss?"

Logan raised his gaze, sorry to see his manager, Vic Downing, standing at the edge of the hawk enclosure. He dropped the tape measure. "What are you still doing here? You should be at home. Tell Vic to go home, Max."

Max, a red-shouldered hawk who was never going to live in the wild again, moved nervously from one foot to the other, head lowered on his flexible neck, fixing Vic with a beady-eyed stare. As if obeying Logan's command, Max let out an ominous screech, the perfect sound track for a horror movie.

Vic just rolled his eyes. "Shut up, pudgy," he said affectionately. It was all an act, of course. Max was gentle-natured, one-winged and a pushover for a fistful of treats. "Look, Logan. I can stay a little while. Let me give you a hand with that."

"You've already worked fifty hours this week. Didn't Gretchen say she'd shoot you if you missed dinner again?"

Vic stuck a piece of Juicy Fruit in his mouth. "Yeah, but that was just the hormones talking." He sighed. "You wouldn't believe how insane pregnant women can be."

Oh, yes, he would. But Logan didn't say that, of course. He also didn't say that Gretchen would undoubtedly get worse in the next few weeks. She had about a month to go, and if Logan remembered correctly from those last months with Rebecca...

But remembering was one thing he didn't waste time doing.

He retrieved his hammer and a broken plank and started working out the nail that was stuck in one end.

"Anyhow," Vic went on, "where I put the bullets, she'll never find them."

Logan looked up. "Where did you hide them?"

"Behind the Windex. Woman hasn't done a lick of housework in months. Says it makes her cranky." Vic tossed down the plank. "But what doesn't?"

As they exchanged a sympathetic chuckle, Logan glimpsed the slow fluttering of something pale and pink at the edge of Vic's silhouette. For a fanciful split second he thought it might be a roseate spoonbill, although he didn't have any at the sanctuary, and undoubtedly never would. The delicate beauties didn't show up this far inland.

He blinked, and the fluttering became the

edges of a loose pink skirt. He blinked again, and saw the woman wearing it.

It was Nora Archer, probably the only woman on the planet who could wear that color with that red hair and pull it off.

She was too far away for Logan to see details, but his mind could conjure up every inch. The silly auburn curls that frothed around her shoulders. The round eyes, too big for her face, forest-colored, mostly brown with shards of green and bronze. Little girl pink cheeks, freckles and an upturned cheerleader's nose. But a dangerous woman's mouth, wide and soft and tempting.

Today, her head was bowed as she moved toward them, her pale face somber. She might have the coloring of a roseate spoonbill, but she had the soft melancholy of the mourning dove.

The widow Archer. He squeezed the handle of the hammer. As beautiful, and as off-limits, as ever.

Vic had noticed her now, too, and both men watched without speaking until she finally reached them. Max stared as well, cocking his head and rotating it slowly to follow her all the way. Logan smiled inwardly. It must be a male thing.

When she got close enough, he stood.

While she was shaking hands with Vic, Logan dropped the hammer again, and brushed his hands against his jeans, sorry that they were gritty with sawdust and dirt.

But that was dumb. His hands were always dirty. The days when he spent all his money on designer suits and weekly manicures were long gone and unlamented.

"Hi, Nora," he said. "I was going to call you again later."

"Logan."

She held out her hand, and he took it. It had been six months, and yet he knew to brace himself for the little electric jolt. She felt it, too, he could tell, though she had always been polished at covering it.

"I came to talk about Sean. To apologize, first of all. He told me what happened this afternoon. He said he did a lot of damage."

"Not so much. He busted up a couple of enclosures. Nothing we can't fix."

Logan was amused to see Vic nodding vigorously, although an hour ago the manager had been ready to wring Sean Archer's neck with his bare hands. That was the effect Nora Archer had on people. Male or female, young or old, one look into those wistful hazel eyes, and they wanted to don armor and jump on a white horse.

She let go of his hand quickly, then gazed around, her lower lip caught between her teeth. "Did he—were there birds in any of the enclosures?"

"The screening wasn't finished yet. It was just bare boards, really. Don't worry, Nora. He hurt stuff, nothing living."

She smiled, still sad but clearly grateful, then turned to Vic. "He tells me you were disturbed about the bird he brought with him. He thinks you believe he killed it."

"Well, I—" Vic looked uncomfortable. "I couldn't be sure. It was dead by the time I got here, and he was kind of going nuts, breaking boards and—"

"I can see why you were worried," she said. "I was worried, too. But I've talked to Sean about it, and he told me everything. I'm convinced he's telling the truth about that part. He simply doesn't have that kind of brutality in him."

Vic didn't look quite as sure, but when he opened his mouth to respond, Johnny Cash's voice suddenly growled out of his back pocket, promising in his rumbling baritone that he found it very, very easy to be true.

Max squawked, disliking the sound instinctively, and Nora's eyes widened.

As the manager dug hurriedly in his back pocket, Logan chuckled. "Vic's cell phone," he explained. "That must be the new ringtone Gretchen put on it. That's not the one that means the baby's coming, is it?"

Vic shook his head. "No. That one's 'Stop, In the Name of Love.' Johnny Cash is the get-your-ass-home-for-dinner ringtone." He clicked the answer button. "Sorry, honey. I know what I said. I'm leaving right now. Yes, right now. No, not five minutes from now. Right now."

Logan pointed at the clinic parking lot, urging the other man to get going. With an apologetic smile and a wave to Nora, Vic loped off toward his truck, keeping his wife updated on every step he took. "I'm ten feet from the truck, honey…"

The few seconds after Vic's departure were subtly awkward. Nora stood in a ray of sunshine that poured in dappled blobs of honey through the oak branches. Logan stood stiffly by the broken wood, in the shadow of the hawk enclosure, surrounded by busted planks and tools.

Well, of course it was awkward. It was the

first time he had been alone with her in about nine months. It was, in fact, only the second time he'd ever been alone with her in his life.

The first time had been at Trent and Susannah's peach party, last summer. They'd had… what…five minutes alone together in the pole shed? Other than that, their encounters had all been casual, public, superficial. The same politely chatting circle at a cocktail party. Nearby tables at a busy café. Two customers apart in the checkout line at the grocery store. Four rows down at the city council meeting.

Funny how you could fool yourself, he thought, watching her scratch an imaginary itch at her throat, then fidget with the neckline of her creamy blouse. The truth was, he hardly knew her. And yet…

"I know you're busy," she said. "I won't take up too much of your time. But I wanted to talk about Sean. I'd like to know what he can do to make this up to you."

"Nothing." He shook his head firmly. "That's not necessary. Let's forget it, okay? I know he's had a hard time this past year."

"Yes. That's true." She swallowed. "I'm sure you've heard all about it. I guess everyone has."

He couldn't deny it. Eastcreek was a typical

small Texas town. People talked. And when they had something juicy to talk about, like the fact that one of its social pillars, Harrison Archer, had gone stark raving mad and tried to kill two people, they buzzed like hornets.

Logan wasn't a fan of gossip. He and Rebecca and Ben had been the subject of enough of it for him to know how little it captured of the real truth. But he couldn't help himself. He had wanted to know. He'd wanted to understand more about that wildly mismatched Archer marriage, so he'd listened.

"I heard. I discounted about half of it, though." He smiled. "I've been here long enough to know that Texans are just as good at embellishing as they are back in Maine."

"In this case, half is bad enough." She moved a little closer to Max's cage, as if she didn't want to meet Logan's eyes while she talked. The hawk, who had been preening his wing, paused briefly, then apparently decided she wasn't a threat and went back to work.

"The basic facts are true. Harrison did threaten to kill Trent and Susannah. He lured Trent out to Green Fern Pond, so that he could shoot him, and when Susannah found them, Harrison held them both at gunpoint. But I don't think he would have done it, even if

Sean...even if Sean hadn't stopped him. I really don't."

She looked back at Logan, her fingertips hooked into the wire screening. "Of course, I don't know for sure. He was very sick, and he was in a lot of pain. He had been for a long time."

He knew she didn't mean physical pain, although that had probably played its part. Pancreatic cancer wasn't a merciful disease. But the pain that had truly destroyed Harrison Archer wasn't the physical kind. It was emotional, and it had apparently eaten away his soul, his conscience and his common sense.

Logan knew he ought to stop her from going on. He didn't have any comfort to offer in return for her confessional. And she didn't need to lay out the details of her private tragedy, like an offering on the altar, buying his forgiveness for Sean.

He'd already forgiven the poor, unlucky kid, for what that was worth.

"You probably know that Harrison blamed Trent for his first son's death." She turned her head back toward the enclosure. Her auburn curls slid across her breastbone, the tips catching the sunlight. "He never got over Paul's death. Not even... Not even after Sean and Harry."

Though many people found that part of the story perplexing, Logan had always sort of understood. The first-born, the miracle, the child of your dreams. You might love again—in fact, humans were probably hardwired to love something, anything, just to survive—but you'd never love like that a second time. Never with your heart wide open, just asking to be smashed to bits.

"Poor Trent." Nora took a deep breath. "He blames himself, too, you know. He shouldn't. Paul died a few years before I came to Eastwood, but from what I hear the fire was just one of those impossibly tragic accidents."

Logan shrugged. "That doesn't make it easier. But you don't have to tell me this, Nora. I think I get it."

"I'd like to explain, if you don't mind listening. I think it might help you to understand Sean a little better."

"Okay."

"Thanks." She gave him a grateful smile. "Anyhow, Harrison had just found out he was dying, and he wanted to avenge Paul's death while he still could. So he...he took Trent out to the pond. It was the last place he'd ever been with Paul. Peggy, Harrison's first wife, called us, and we came as fast as we could. We had no idea what we would find. And Sean…he ran ahead…"

She'd been telling the story with impressive composure so far. But finally, when she spoke about Sean, her voice trembled. Her eyes were shining, anguished, the muscles around them pulled so tight it hurt to see.

He picked up the hammer again and inspected the handle, which had felt a little loose when he was working earlier. He needed to resist this irrational urge to move toward her.

What was he going to do? Take her in his arms?

Oh, man. This was why he'd decided it was better to steer clear of her. There was something about her that wormed straight into the weakest chink inside him.

What exactly was her magic? She was small, only about five-four, he'd guess barely a hundred pounds. Nice figure, but she'd never stop traffic. She wore almost no jewelry or makeup, didn't bother with ornamentation. She was soft-spoken and introspective.

She should have been easy to ignore.

And yet, ever since he'd moved to Texas eighteen months ago, he hadn't been able to get her out of his mind. Not then, when she'd been a meekly married woman, clearly in the no-touch zone. And not now, when she was the epitome of Mrs. Wrong: a single mother with troubled sons. Vulnerable, grief-stricken and needy. Oddly innocent, incapable of the kind of no-strings fling he specialized in.

"Look, it's really okay," he said gruffly, trying to ignore the tenderness that was threatening to create itself inside him. Her problems were her problems. He couldn't solve them. Hell, he couldn't even solve his own. "I'm not mad at Sean, and the damage is easily enough repaired."

"That's very generous." She finally turned completely around. Max grumbled, sorry to lose the attention, and the hope of a treat. "But, for Sean's sake, I have to do more. I can't let him get away with this. He needs to pay for what he's done."

Logan felt his chest tighten. He didn't like where this was going.

"I'll send you a bill. You can make him work it off. You know. Chores around the house. Teach him his lesson."

She moved a step toward him. "That seems so remote from the crime, though, don't you think? Is there any work he could do at the sanctuary? It would teach him so much more. He'd learn what you do here, for one thing. Surely, if he understood that what you do is so valuable, so unlike what his fa—"

She broke off awkwardly. But he knew what she meant.

Harrison Archer, whose family tree had put its roots down in Texas before it was even called Texas, had never thought much of Easterners, and he damn sure didn't think much of wasting a hundred acres of prime horse and cattle country to nurse a bunch of half-dead hawks and barn owls back to health.

He'd undoubtedly passed that disdain on to his son, the heir-in-training to all the Archer arrogance. Logan hadn't connected the father's attitude to Sean's outburst, but perhaps Nora was right. If Sean hadn't heard so much at home about how worthless Two Wings was, the urge to do it violence might not have been so close to the surface.

"You've got a point," Logan said, trying to sound reasonable. "It would be nice to have next-door neighbors who don't think Two Wings is a waste of space. But I'm afraid Sean's re-education will have to be done at home. We have only about six weeks before we open Two Wings to the public, and I'm just too busy to play guidance counselor, or parole officer, or whatever you're thinking."

"No, I didn't mean you. Of course you don't have time."

Her eyes had clouded again, and he realized his rejection had been more forceful than he'd intended. *Damn it.* Why couldn't he reach equilibrium with this woman? Why couldn't she just be another pretty neighbor? Why did the idea of having her, and her little boy, at Two Wings every day make him so uncomfortable?

"I meant your manager. Do you think Vic might have time? I promise you, Sean can be a hard worker. He's smart and he's strong."

Logan had started shaking his head when she began to talk, and he didn't stop. She frowned, clearly wondering why his resistance was so absolute.

"And of course I'd be happy," she said cautiously, "to make a donation to Two Wings, to offset whatever inconvenience or expense Sean's presence might create."

"I don't want your money."

Crap. That had come out too harshly, too, especially given the obvious differences in their financial states. *Smooth, Cathcart. Whip out the whole bag of insecurities, why don't you? Want to tell her about the puppy that died when you were two?*

She studied him for a minute, her wide forehead knitting between the brows. "What's really the matter, Logan? Do you think Sean killed that bird? Is that why you don't want him here? You're afraid he's crazy?"

"No. Of course not. No."

For a minute he considered telling the truth. She knew he was attracted to her, and vice versa. It had never been put into words, but it was as obvious as a neon sign. Would it be so bad to just talk about it?

But what exactly would he say? *I'm not interested in a long-term relationship with a woman like you, but as you know I'm wildly turned on by you anyhow. I'm afraid that if we spend too much time together, I might seduce you, and I might end up breaking your heart....*

Yeah, right.

Not in this lifetime.

Besides, the attraction was only part of the problem.

The rest of it was that he just didn't want to get involved in the Archer family tragedy. Call him a selfish bastard, but he didn't want to feel their pain. He didn't want to dig around in the muck of their grief and see if he could help them drain the swamp. He didn't want to lend his ear, offer his shoulder or hold the Kleenex while they cried.

He couldn't help them anyhow. Bereavement wasn't like some club you joined. There wasn't a secret handshake he could show them, no guided tour he could lead to help them feel at home.

It was a private hell, and everyone was locked up in their own solitary fire.

"I'm sorry, Nora," he said. He picked up the tool box to show that he was out of time. "I'm afraid there's nothing I can do."

Chapter Three

"Jeepers, Nora. I asked you to come because I wanted to talk about Sean. But now I think we'd better talk about you, instead." Jolie Harper, the music teacher at Eastcreek Elementary School, leaned forward, elbows on her desk. "You look awful. Aren't you sleeping?"

"Not much." Nora plopped into the visitor's seat, relieved to be able to drop the brave face for once. She had volunteered in Jolie's classroom several times a week for the past three years, and had come to trust her completely.

"I try to sleep, but my mind won't shut off. I keep second-guessing every decision I make. I've told Sean he'll have to work off the damage to the Cathcart place. But am I being too hard on him? Too soft? Does he need more freedom? Less? Evelyn thinks—"

"Ugh. Spare me what Evelyn thinks."

Jolie stood and went to the window. Using her thumb and forefinger, she wedged a crack in the blinds so that she could peek into the rehearsal room, where her assistant was helping Sean and three other students learn "The Star Spangled Banner" on the guitar, flute, clarinet and bells.

She grimaced. "They sound terrible. Any chance they'd let us have our spring show in August this year?"

Nora smiled, although the joke, obviously meant to lighten the tension, paradoxically set off a new pang of guilt. The guitar was another former love that Sean no longer enjoyed. Getting him to practice was like pulling teeth, and half the time Nora just didn't think it was worth the struggle.

They couldn't fight all day, every day, could they? What kind of life would that be for a nine-year-old boy?

Or was she taking the easy way out, craving peace, even at her son's expense?

She reached up and rubbed her aching forehead. This was the kind of emotional tail-chasing that kept her up all night. For Evelyn, life was so straightforward. In her opinion, Nora was a naive woman who had no idea how to steer her sons through this dangerous storm and should rely on Evelyn for guidance. End of debate.

In those sleepless hours before dawn, Nora sometimes wondered if she might be right.

"So why did you ask me to come in, Jolie?" She braced herself. She might as well know the worst. "Has something else happened?"

Jolie cast one more glance into the rehearsal room. Apparently satisfied that Sean was safely occupied, she leaned against the edge of her desk, close enough to speak softly and still be heard.

"Not really. Nothing dramatic. It's just that… he seems very remote. He doesn't volunteer for anything extra, doesn't go for the chair challenges. He doesn't hang out with his friends much, either. He sits by himself whenever he has a choice. He doesn't cause trouble. He just doesn't…" She sighed. "Doesn't engage."

Nora laced her fingers in her lap and squeezed tightly. Out of nowhere, she felt the urge to talk to Harrison. She would like his advice, of course, but she'd also like to be able to tell him that she understood so much better what he'd been through with Paul.

Intellectually, any human being could grasp that it was terrible to watch your son suffer and die. Anyone with a heart could sympathize with a tragedy like that.

But when you actually went through it, when the fear that your child might be hurting, might be in danger, ran through your veins like a fiery poison, threatening to blow your heart up right in your chest…that was a whole new level of understanding.

"I see that apathy at home, too," she said. "At first I thought it might be an improvement, a sign that he was calming down. But it's not natural. It's too bottled up."

"Right." Jolie's shiny blond ponytail bounced jauntily as she nodded, but her face was very serious. "Like a fire behind a tightly closed door." She glanced toward the window again. "Is he still seeing the counselor?"

"Yes, but he's down to once a week. It was the psychiatrist's suggestion. He said it was time to move toward normalcy. I thought it might be too soon, but he said we should try."

Evelyn had pooh-poohed Nora's doubts, eager to accept the psychiatrist's recommendation. The older woman didn't set much store by talk therapy, which she believed encouraged brooding on your troubles, instead of moving past them. She called it "wallowing."

"I'll phone him tomorrow." Just making the decision loosened the knot in Nora's chest slightly. She leaned back in the chair and took a deep breath. The varied scents of the classroom were soothing to her. The sharp, alcohol sting of whiteboard markers, the crisp sweetness of new textbooks, the warm musk of children.

And best of all, the muted laughter of students in the next room struggling to make music.

She'd always planned to be a music teacher, like Jolie. She loved working with kids, watching them light up as their clumsy efforts suddenly bloomed into beautiful sounds.

When she first went to visit Harrison at the Bull's Eye Ranch that summer ten years ago, she'd been only twenty-one, just out of college, still interviewing for teaching positions in South Carolina. By the time she landed a job, she knew she might be pregnant. And by the time classes started in South Carolina that September, she was living in Texas, married to a very rich man twice her age.

Harrison quickly quieted her talk of teaching. Motherhood, he insisted, was a full-time job.

Understanding why he was a bit overprotective, she'd indulged him. He'd bought her a beautiful piano, so that she could keep up with her own music, and she'd appreciated the gesture.

Someday, she'd always promised herself, she'd start over. When the boys were older. When Harrison felt more secure—about her, and about them. She'd earn her Texas certification, and she'd finally stand in her very own classroom.

Guess *someday* was on permanent hold now.

And she didn't mind. There was only one goal that mattered anymore. Shepherding what was left of her family through this crisis.

But she didn't want her worries to monopolize this whole visit. Jolie had problems, too.

"So did the PTA finally agree that you need new sheet music?" Nora knew that the recent budget cutbacks had slashed the school arts programs. Jolie would have had to cancel the Independence Day concert if Nora hadn't written a personal check for new instruments. She'd write another, if the PTA didn't come through with funds. She might write one, anyhow. One of the nicer aspects of having money was being able to give it away.

"It's still under advisement." Jolie rolled her eyes. "Which means they're waiting to see what the Phys Ed teacher needs. If it's a choice between music and sports, we all know who—"

Suddenly, midsentence, she lurched forward, though she must have been reacting to some sixth sense. Nora hadn't noticed anything amiss.

"Oh, dear Lord," Jolie murmured under her breath. She flung open the door to the rehearsal room. "Madeline, grab Sean."

Nora was only a foot behind her, so she had just entered the room when Sean's guitar hit the floor. Obviously the instrument had been flung with force. Contact with the linoleum made a hideous sound, part splintering wood, part ghastly harmonies from reverberating strings.

"Oh, Sean, no," she said softly.

Her son didn't hear her. He stood on the other side of the room, rigid as a pole, his eyes sparking with fury. His face shone palely, which made his freckles stand out like copper pennies on his cheeks. His hair was mussed, his collar lifted where Madeline, the assistant music instructor, held it in her fist.

Jolie had one hand lightly but authoritatively placed on the shoulder of a second boy. Nora knew him—Tad Rutherford. He and Sean had played together since the kiddie band in nursery school. Tad was Sean's age, but twice his size, and something of a bully. Right now, his broad face burned red, his breath coming hard and noisy.

Nora's heart beat high in her chest. But Jolie, as always, looked completely calm, in spite of the chaos, the wild-eyed boys and the smashed guitar, which was now two splintered halves held together only by the strings.

She owned the situation. She had frozen the potential for trouble right in its tracks with just the force of her silent authority. That was her gift. It made her a wonderful teacher.

She glanced at Sean, then at Tad. "What happened here?"

"I was just kidding," Tad said, his chest still heaving. "I didn't mean it."

"Didn't mean what?"

Flushing brightly, Tad ducked his head and stared at his shoes. Whatever he'd said, he didn't seem to have the courage to repeat it in front of the adults.

Jolie looked across the room. "Sean?"

Sean didn't flinch away from her gaze. He met it, his jaw squared so tightly he might have been carved from marble—if it hadn't been for his eyes, which were alive with emotion.

Jolie's gaze shifted. "Madeline?"

The assistant shook her head. "They were playing. I didn't hear it."

Jolie didn't waste time with the third degree. She obviously knew what had to be done. She walked over to Nora. Her eyes were sympathetic, but her voice was matter-of-fact.

"I'll have to call the principal," she said quietly, touching the phone that hung from her belt. "The rules are very clear."

Nora understood. "Of course."

Nodding to her assistant, a message that seemed to speak volumes, Jolie slipped back into her office to make the call. Nora moved slowly to her son's side, sidestepping the wreckage of the guitar.

"Sean." She knelt in front of him and took his cold, limp hand. "Honey, can you tell me? Can you tell me what happened?"

For a moment he stared at her. And then, slowly, as if his neck were a rusted joint, he shook his head.

Such an absolute silence. She looked into

his eyes, where sparks of fury still flashed and simmered.

And she thought of Jolie's comment.

Like fire, she thought with a sinking heart. Like fire behind a tightly closed door.

Logan's night had been an unexpected success. Dinner and drinks with Annie... Aden? Arden? Something like that. The office manager for one of the vets he used at Two Wings.

He'd asked her out purely because she was smoking hot, and he was bored with the book he'd been reading. But he got the bonus prize, too. She'd turned out to be witty and sensible, and extremely easy to please. She liked her steak, she liked her wine. She liked his jokes, his car, his jacket and his smile.

It was also pretty clear she liked the idea of coming home with him. It should have been a slam dunk—sex with a woman who was easy to please. And did he mention smoking hot?

But for some reason he would never understand, he ignored all the signals, kissed her politely at her door and drove back to Two Wings alone.

He didn't try to figure himself out. He'd never been into navel-gazing self-analysis. He was tired. Her perfume turned him off. He hadn't been in the mood for a blonde. Whatever.

What difference did it make? There was always another night. There was always another Annie.

He poured himself a glass of water and picked up the sports section, which he hadn't had time to read that morning. He kicked off his shoes and, with a satisfied yawn, settled onto the tweedy sofa that faced the picture window. It was only eleven, but he'd been up since five, and he'd be up again at five tomorrow. He was dog tired, and he had a right to be.

When the doorbell rang two minutes later, he cursed under his breath. But he swung his legs off the sofa and tossed the newspaper onto the floor. It might be someone dropping off a bird.

When he opened the door, at first he didn't see anyone at all. Then his gaze fell about two feet, and he discovered a kid standing there, the pale oval of his face peering out from a black hooded sweatshirt.

He wore black jeans, too, and black sneakers. He looked like a miniature cat burglar.

"Hi, Sean," Logan said wryly. "Did we have something else you wanted to bust up?"

The boy flushed, but he covered it well with

a deep scowl. "My mom says she's going to pay you for it. She's making me work it off. I'm going to have to pull weeds about ten hours a day for a month."

"Good." Logan kept his hand on the doorknob, but he scanned the driveway for a car. "Is your mom with you now?"

"No. I came alone. On my bike."

Oh, great. The moron had ridden a mile and a half in the pitch dark. All in black. Probably didn't even have a light on his bike.

He needed a good shaking. Didn't he have the slightest idea what it would do to his mother if anything bad happened to him?

"Does she know you're here?"

"No. She's out with my Aunt Evelyn. I didn't climb out my window this time. I went straight out the front door. Milly's supposed to be looking after me, but she always falls asleep. She's got blood sugar."

"Really." Logan fought the urge to smile. "Well, I'm afraid I'm going to have to take you back, then. If Milly wakes up and finds you gone, she'll have a heart attack to go with her blood sugar."

"No. It's okay. She never wakes up. I'm not going back yet."

Logan looked at the boy, who clearly had

amazing persistence and dogged determination in that stubborn jaw.

He did some quick thinking. He didn't want to spook the kid. If Sean decided to dart off into the night, in that outfit, Logan would have hell's own time trying to catch him. He was tired, and barefoot, and about twenty years older than Sean. He didn't like his chances.

"Okay." He held open the door. "Want to come in, then?"

Sean hesitated, still frowning. He glanced into the lighted great room, as if he were checking for trap doors and cages.

"Hey, suit yourself," Logan said, chuckling. Kids were so dumb. Sean had snuck out in the middle of the night, wandered the darkness alone, knocked on a stranger's door, then suddenly started remembering what Mom said about safety first.

He shrugged. "I have all the snotty kid prisoners I need at the moment, anyhow."

Sean laughed. It was an awkward, sputtering noise, as if he hadn't expected to, and hadn't wanted to. He caught himself and cut it off, but it had undoubtedly been a laugh.

Encouraged, Logan opened the door wider, and ambled casually toward the kitchen. "Want some water? Must have been a dusty ride. Did you come the back way, by the creek?"

Behind him, he heard the door shut softly. Then he heard it open again, and once more click shut. Too funny…the kid must have been testing to make sure it didn't auto-lock.

The soft slap of sneakers followed him to the kitchen. Then Sean spoke, with the belligerence dialed back a notch. "Water would be very nice. Yeah, I came by the creek. It's nice in the moonlight."

Logan slid a filled glass across the countertop. "But it's a long way. And I'm guessing that if you get caught you're in a boatload of trouble. What do you want so bad you're willing to come all this way to get it?"

Sean picked up the water and swallowed about half of it before he answered. "I want the bird," he said. "I was going to go to the center and poke around till I found it, but that seemed babyish."

He lifted his small, pale chin. The hood dropped off when he did so, exposing his curly red hair, still sweaty from the ride over. "And I'm not a baby. So I decided I'd come ask you for it. You can't want it. It's not worth anything."

In spite of the absurdity of the situation,

Logan felt a stirring of respect. The boy's behavior didn't make any sense, and he could definitely use an attitude adjustment.

But that didn't make it any less brave.

"I'm not sure I understand. What bird?"

"The one I brought over here yesterday."

"The dead one?"

The scowl appeared again. "It wasn't dead when I left my house. It flew right into my window, and then it couldn't fly anymore. I thought maybe you could fix it. But I guess I took too long. When I got here, it was already dead." His fingertips were white where they gripped the glass. "I... I couldn't believe it. It just wasn't breathing."

Logan watched the boy carefully, recognizing that helpless anger, that bewildered impotence in the face of the implacability of mortality. If he'd had any doubts before about Sean's culpability in the death of the bird, they vanished now.

"I guess that was a pretty bad moment. When you saw that it was too late."

"Yeah." Sean had to take a deep breath to stop his voice from quavering. "Yeah, it was. I wanted to save it. Maybe it was even my fault. Maybe if I'd asked my mom to drive me over—"

"No." Logan couldn't allow that thought to exist for a single second. "No. If it flew into your window, it probably broke its neck. No matter how fast you got it here, I couldn't have saved it, either."

"Okay." Sean nodded, staring down at his water. "But your manager took it away from me. I don't want him just thrown in the trash, you know? I want to bury him. But I don't want to steal him. I shouldn't have to. He's mine."

He lifted his head and stood ramrod straight. All the regal Archer entitlement was in that bearing, but so was the little boy's fear and confusion. Those angry eyes were shining with unshed tears. The effect was incongruous, and oddly touching.

"So I thought I'd come over here and ask you straight. Will you let me have his body?"

Goddamn it. For a minute Logan felt his own eyes stinging. *Damn it.* He was not going to actually go soft over this kid and one silly bird. Birds died on him all the time in the sanctuary. No one wept over it, not even the most naive teenage volunteers.

"I can't," he said firmly. Facts were facts. "I'm sorry, but at least I can promise you it wasn't thrown in the trash. We've already incinerated the body. We have to do that to all the birds we lose here at Two Wings. It's the law."

"Oh." Sean bit his lips together, dealing with the disappointment. His throat worked a few seconds as he fought for control. "Why?"

He really seemed to want to know. Logan debated with himself for a second—would it be better to gloss over it, or offer up details as a distraction?

He decided on distraction. He simplified, but he laid out the basic setup, the federal laws that governed rehabbers and sanctuaries like Two Wings. Encouraged by Sean's absorbed attention, he even included some interesting trivia about how hunters used to kill birds by the thousands because women wanted to wear their elegant nesting plumage in their ridiculous hats.

"There was a period, maybe a hundred years ago, when an ounce of ostrich feathers was worth more than an ounce of gold," he finished up. "So the government passed laws to protect the birds. We aren't allowed to keep so much as a single feather."

The stories, and the time it took to tell them, did the trick. By the time Logan was finished, Sean's eyes were brighter. The lightening of his fog of unhappiness was palpable. He probably didn't fully understand most of it, but he was clearly fascinated by the brief glimpse of the rich history of bird lore.

Logan looked him over, above the rim of his own water glass. When Sean stopped all that glowering, he was a fairly nice-looking kid.

"Anyhow, I really should get you home now," Logan said casually, hoping he wouldn't rekindle the fire. "Think we can get your bike in the back of my truck?"

Sean nodded reluctantly. Whatever adrenaline had pushed him here was fading now that his anger and tension were gone. He was starting to look like a normal, sleepy little boy.

"Thanks," Sean said. "Thanks for being so nice to me."

And then, to Logan's surprise, Sean suddenly thrust out his hand. Logan took it, feeling the fragile bones in the skinny fingers, and the calluses on his fingertips. The hand felt ridiculously small to be offering such a man's gesture.

"You're welcome," Logan said, but he had to clear his throat to get the words out.

"I won't bother you any more, Mr. Cathcart." The boy looked him straight in the eye. "I'm sorry I lost my temper yesterday and messed up your cages. I wish I could do something to take it back."

Logan felt himself being drawn into those hazel eyes, so round and so much like his mother's. He was no psychiatrist, but his instincts told him this kid wasn't crazy, or mean, or bad. He was just hurting like hell.

Oh, man. Logan felt himself about to say something he'd probably regret. *Pull back, Cathcart. Think it through.*

Remember the attitude. The flash of temper. The tragedy, hanging like a black wing over everything the boy did. Remember that half his DNA was from his dad, who had always been a jerk, and had ended up a head case.

Everything he'd told himself yesterday was still true. He still had too much to do. He still knew Nora's sex appeal would be a distraction, an itch he could never scratch.

And he damn sure still didn't want to jump on the Archer family trouble train.

Besides, would working at the sanctuary really be helpful for Sean? True, Logan honored hard, outdoor, sweaty work, and he believed in the therapeutic value of getting in touch with, and resigning yourself to, the rhythms of nature.

But this was a kid with death issues. A kid

who would try to save his dad all over again every time he tried to save a bird. And lose his dad all over again every time he failed.

Logan wasn't up to dealing with that. Just because, for a minute here, Sean reminded him of Nora, of the forest-colored sadness in her eyes…

That was no reason to—

He tried to apply the brakes, but nothing seemed to have the power to stop the skid.

"That's the rotten thing about mistakes," he said, testing to see whether Sean's belligerence had really subsided. "Once you make 'em, you own 'em. You can't take them back, no matter how much you want to."

Sean nodded grimly, but no resentment sparked. "Yeah." He sighed. "It sucks."

Logan paused one more time, giving himself another second to come to his senses.

But it didn't happen.

"I tell you what," he heard himself saying. "Maybe there is something you could do. Why don't we see if your mom will let you work off your punishment here with me?"

Chapter Four

The sky was already a hot neon blue by eight o'clock when Sean reported for his first shift at the sanctuary on Saturday. More like summer than spring, really, Nora thought as she parked the car by the double row of hackberry trees, where the dappled trees would keep it cool.

She didn't know how long she'd be staying. She'd expected to drop Sean off and return for him later, but as they neared the small wooden cabin that housed the sanctuary's reception area, Sean's shoulders grew rigid and his lower jaw thrust out.

Nora knew those signs. He was scared, but tightening every muscle to avoid showing it.

"You're coming in, too, right, Mom?"

"Of course."

"Good." His shoulders loosened, and he gave her a shrug that said the whole thing bored him. "Mr. Cathcart's probably forgotten I'm coming, anyhow."

Nora bit back a frustrated response. She wished she knew how to prevent Sean from masking his fear with belligerence, but Harrison had worked hard to be sure his son and heir knew better than to show weakness. Probably the lesson of his own father, Harrison believed that anger was the manly man's only respectable emotion.

It would take more than a few months with a child psychiatrist to make Sean disloyal to his father's teachings now.

But the night Logan had brought Sean home, his bike in the flatbed of a Two Wings truck, had given her a glimmer of hope.

They'd rung the bell politely, and then Logan had stood with his hand on the boy's shoulder, as if to lend moral support, while Sean had explained about sneaking out to retrieve the body of the bird.

Nora had hardly recognized her son that night. No stubborn silence, no slippery fibs, no tantrums. Just the truth, offered somberly, even apologetically, with a glimpse of the grown man he would someday be.

She'd kept her own tone equally forthright, though she couldn't pretend she wasn't upset, or that there wouldn't be a punishment.

Then, together, the three of them had come up with this plan.

It called for Sean to work at Two Wings three hours every Saturday morning, and two hours every Monday, Wednesday and Friday until the damage was paid off.

His salary would be five dollars an hour. Logan had estimated the damage at five hundred dollars, though Nora suspected him of minimizing the mess. Still, Sean would clearly be working into the summer. That night, he'd seemed reconciled to the plan.

But as the first day grew closer, his anxiety had increased, and out came the attitude. By this morning, he'd been sullen, difficult to rouse. He "lost" the green Two Wings T-shirt Logan had provided, groused about the jeans and sneakers his volunteer training sheet called for, and presented himself at the breakfast table with a scowl and no appetite.

She had a feeling Logan was going to regret his decision to bring Sean on board.

"See?" Sean shoved his car door shut, then

looked around the empty parking lot. "Told you he forgot. There's no one here."

"Maybe we're early."

But she saw his point. Two Wings seemed deserted. The only sounds were the sawing of unseen crickets, the croaking of invisible frogs and the occasional melodic whistle of birds that flitted between the trees.

The ticket window, still unmarked awaiting the formal opening of the sanctuary to the public, was firmly shut, reflecting back only the blue sky and the ancient trees.

"He's probably in the clinic," she said, trying to remember how to get to the main part of the sanctuary. In the eighteen months since Logan Cathcart had moved in, she'd only been here once, the day she came to apologize for Sean's vandalism.

She knew the general layout of the land, because she used to visit often when it was owned by Logan's great-aunt, Doreen Cathcart. Doreen had been eccentric, but a kind woman. She'd never liked Harrison, who thought her land was wasted and wanted to buy it. But she'd always welcomed Nora and the boys.

The house was over on the western edge of the property. On the other side, Doreen had built an odd little amphitheater. She'd hoped to turn the whole estate into a performance arts center, but the dream died with the amphitheater when the money ran out.

"He might be back where those big enclosures are," she said, trying to orient herself now. "I went down that little boardwalk, off to the left."

He seemed unsure whether he should admit that he knew where that was.

She waited.

"Okay, fine. It's back here." Sean moved to the left, where the wooden boardwalk snaked through the trees.

He obviously knew his way well, and she wondered how often he might have been here. He'd been caught twice now, but was that all?

A chill crept through her as she watched him walk confidently through the heavily wooded maze, never hesitating when the boardwalk forked off in different directions.

How many lies had he been telling her? Would she have to take all freedom away from him? Was there to be no more fun, no more riding his bike with his friend Paddy James, or helping the ranch hands with the horses? Would she have to peek into his room every few minutes when he played video games, or did his homework, or even while he slept?

Would she ever be able to trust him again?

As they walked, birdcalls grew louder, and after a couple of hundred yards, the trees thinned and the path ended in a large open area filled with huge, screened-in wood pens.

And Nora saw that Two Wings was far from empty.

It bustled with life.

The enclosures were filled with hawks and eagles and owls and vultures. That didn't surprise her. She'd seen them last week.

But, unlike last week, the place was teeming with human life, too.

At least half a dozen people moved purposefully about, ignoring the concrete paths and taking shortcuts across the sand and grass. They lugged hoses and bags of feed, rakes and brooms and boards. One man carried a large hawklike bird on his gloved hand.

"Sean. Good. You made it."

Logan's voice brought Nora out of her dazed surprise. She'd completely misunderstood the scale of the place. Harrison had always been so dismissive that she'd assumed Two Wings must be some kind of dilettante's hobby.

But this was no hobby. This was a mission.

Logan nodded at Nora. "Thanks for bringing him. See you at eleven?"

She felt Sean tense up beside her. She smiled at Logan, hoping he'd understand. "I'm sorry to be the hovering mother, but could you show me a little of what Sean will be doing while he's here?"

Logan didn't exactly look delighted, though he was too nice a man to refuse, no matter how busy he was.

"No problem," he said. "But remember it's not glamorous." He held out his hands, which were stained and gritty. "We've been spreading mulch. To tell you the truth, I'm going to be darn glad to let Sean take over."

"Mulch?" Sean scowled. "I thought I'd be working with the birds."

"Sean," Nora admonished. "You'll do whatever Mr. Cathcart—"

"No," Logan said bluntly. "You won't be working with the birds yet. You won't be doing anything alone. We don't take regular volunteers under the age of eighteen, so you're kind of a special case. Todd or Matt will work with you. They're good. You'll learn a lot from them."

"I think I can clean out a bunch of cages." Sean frowned. "I'm not an idiot."

"No, but you're a beginner. Beginners make mistakes, and either they get hurt, or the birds do."

Sean's mouth was still set hard, but after a couple of seconds of trying to stare Logan down, he blinked first. He lowered his gaze, toeing the sand with his sneaker.

"Yeah," he said under his breath. "Fine."

Nora's cheeks burned, but Logan didn't seem overly concerned about his new volunteer's attitude. Maybe he'd expected nothing better. That was probably why he'd been so reluctant to let Sean participate. He undoubtedly knew he'd have to assign someone to follow the boy around like a nanny, to be sure he didn't do something dumb.

Or just plain run away.

Logan might have said he didn't want a donation from her, but she suddenly saw that it would take a mighty big check to compensate for the hassle Sean was likely going to be.

Scattered among the large bird enclosures were several small, neat, officelike buildings. Logan began leading them toward the one marked Clinic. Off to the side of that building, a couple of teenagers were scattering handfuls of dark chips that smelled like pine-bark mulch.

"Hey, Mark. Todd." Logan waved toward the teens. "Come meet Sean—"

But at that moment a young girl's head

poked out of the clinic door. "Logan, the vet's on the phone. He's in a hurry, but he says Fritz is ready, and he needs to talk to you about Punk."

Logan nodded. "Thanks, Dolly. I'll take it." He looked at Nora. She thought it might be time to depart. She was about to open her mouth and say so when he suddenly cocked his head. "Want to see one of our permanent residents?"

She looked at Sean, but he deliberately turned his head, just to show how unimpressed he was.

She smiled at Logan apologetically. "If it's not too much trouble, that would be very cool."

The clinic was small, more like a condo kitchenette than a vet's office. When all four of them bundled inside, and Logan made quick introductions, there wasn't much room to spare.

She usually avoided being this close, physically, to Logan. She never sat next to him at meetings, or gave him the same casual hug she might have given any other acquaintance she met on the street.

It was partly because of Harrison's suspicions. But it was also a self-protective choice. As absurd as it sounded for a thirty-two-year-old housewife, Logan Cathcart gave her butterflies.

She wasn't really sure why. Though he was amazing to look at, with his dark hair, his intense blue eyes and his six feet of lean muscle, she was completely immune to a hundred men equally well-endowed.

But Logan's masculinity obviously transmitted on her frequency, and she wasn't sure she ever completely concealed the jitters. The best bet had seemed to be maintaining a cordial distance.

Today, though, in such cramped quarters, she didn't have much choice. And, with her emotions so caught up in Sean's problems, anything as frivolous as butterflies seemed unlikely. She just tried to stay out of anyone's way.

"Kind of messy, isn't it?" Sean let his scornful gaze drift over the cupboards and bookshelves that lined the walls, overflowing with medical tomes and binders from various federal and state agencies.

"Sean," she said, her voice stiff with warning.

Logan chuckled as he took the phone from Dolly. "Yeah, it's a mess, all right. Maybe that would be a good job for you tomorrow."

In the corner, hand puppets that looked like birds had been tossed into a basket. Sean went over to inspect them, but tossed each one back indifferently, as if they didn't pass the test. Dolly ignored him, fiddling with instruments that looked like tiny forceps.

Logan's phone call was brief, a few monosyllabic words that seemed to indicate satisfaction. Apparently the vet's news was good, though Nora wondered how often that was the case. Surely not all the birds brought here found happy endings.

She looked at Sean, his tense, bony shoulders and his unruly red hair that stood up in a tuft at the part. For a minute she saw him as another of Logan's wounded birds, and wondered whether he would be one of the lucky ones.

"Sorry about that." Logan joined them at the counter. "The vets we use are all volunteers, so I had to catch him while he was free. Dolly, I'll weigh Gulliver today. If you could make sure the status sheets in the pens are ready, that would be great."

The young woman, whose hair was brown with purple tips, and whose nose was decorated with a serious piece of hardware, smiled amiably.

"Sure thing, boss," she said, waving at Nora and Sean before skipping out the door and down the path toward the larger enclosures.

Logan moved to the farthest countertop, where cages stood in rows next to large scales and microscopes and first aid supplies.

"Gulliver is one of the birds we're going to use for education," Logan said as he opened a large gray cage and peeked in. "Hey, buddy," he said to whatever occupant waited inside. "Time to see how fat you're getting, living the life of leisure."

He put his hand in slowly, and when he pulled it out, he held the most adorable piece of brown-and-white fluff Nora had ever seen. She smiled instinctively, and when she glanced at Sean, she saw that his scowl had deepened, which she knew meant he was working hard to suppress his curiosity.

"Oh, how darling," she said. "Sean, look! It's a baby owl!"

Sean moved dramatically away, sighing to communicate his boredom. But he remained angled, so that he could still glimpse the little bird out of the corners of his eyes.

Of course he was fascinated. How could he not be?

The owl was so cute Nora had to laugh.

About six inches long, it fit neatly in the palm of Logan's large hand.

And then the hand itself was almost too much of a distraction. It was definitely not a rancher's hand, with its graceful, long lines. She was surprised to see the elegant fingers tipped in calluses.

Sean made an impatient sound as he toyed with the instruments on the counter.

"I thought," he said, "that you weren't supposed to let them see people much, so that they don't imprint on humans."

Nora gave her son a hard look, and she was glad to see that he flushed, obviously aware that his tone had been out of bounds. What made him think he could teach Logan his own business?

"Been reading up?" Logan nodded, as if he approved. "You're right. For a baby, we'd have to wear the puppet, or even the whole outfit. But Gulliver here isn't a baby. He's a fully grown Eastern screech owl, and unfortunately somebody already let him imprint on humans before he got to us."

"But he's so small," Nora said. "He's fully grown?"

"I know." Logan scratched the side of the bird's head. The owl seemed quite content to lounge in his hand, blinking its large, shiny eyes at him sleepily. "They don't get much bigger than this. And they don't screech, either. Weird, huh?"

Sean was no longer pretending not to watch. His hands were fisted at chest level, as if he had to force himself not to reach out and touch the intricately patterned feathers.

Nora met Logan's gaze over her son's head. She wondered if he knew how embarrassed she was by Sean's behavior.

Or how worried.

But she couldn't read anything in Logan's blue eyes except a polite patience.

"I should probably get going," she said.

She should. She had a million things to do, and she was postponing the moment when Sean would have to adjust. Maybe, when the safety net that Mommy provided was gone, he'd settle down and behave.

If he didn't, she knew it wouldn't be long before Logan kicked his surly attitude out of here. Two Wings wasn't occupational therapy for bratty boys. This was, as she'd observed earlier, a mission.

Logan Cathcart cared about this place and these birds. He wouldn't waste much time on a nasty kid who didn't understand that.

So she needed to let them get to work.

She moved toward the door.

"I'll be back at eleven, Sean, all right?" She put her hand on the knob.

"I guess." Sean stood stiffly.

She opened the door, looking over her shoulder. To her surprise, Logan was watching her, his hand gently holding the ball of fluff in place on the scale.

When she hesitated, his eyes softened, and he nodded briefly. The gesture was oddly comforting.

It'll be okay, that nod seemed to say. *I'll take care of him.*

She might be imagining it. God knew she'd imagined a lot of things about Logan Cathcart over the past eighteen months. Things that weren't real, and never would be.

But, as she let the door shut behind her and made her way back to the parking lot, she realized she felt a whole lot better anyhow.

Sean's first week was a disaster.

It was a battle to get him to Two Wings every time. He complained bitterly, inventing a hundred obstacles. A test he absolutely had to study for. A blistered finger. An extra Little League practice.

Somehow, Nora held her ground, though when she presented him to Vic Downing, who seemed to have taken over nanny duty, she felt as if she were handing off a piece of dynamite, set to blow at any minute.

She never saw Logan, though she would have liked to thank him, and get his read on Sean's chances of settling in.

Logan's absence had to be deliberate. She assumed he didn't want to have to say things that would hurt her. And he didn't want to have to lie.

Every day when she picked Sean up, then drove him home in sour silence, she expected a call from Logan before the night was over.

He might try to gloss it over, if he felt kind. He might create some excuse that didn't sound as if he were rejecting her son.

Or maybe he'd just tell it straight. They couldn't handle Sean's tempers or his arrogance.

Either way, she couldn't blame him. Sean's behavior had never been worse. He obviously hated the menial tasks Logan assigned him, and he resented being bossed around by the senior volunteers.

But, amazingly, the call never came.

The following Monday, when the boys were

at school, she headed into town to proof the programs she'd designed for Jolie's spring concert.

Because Harrison had insisted she stay at home with the boys instead of working, Nora had always been vigorously involved with the PTA. Over the years, she'd become fairly decent at designing flyers, newsletters, brochures and concert programs. The other parents considered her the go-to person for such things, and she welcomed the creative outlet.

Jasper's was the only printer in Eastcreek proper, so she knew she might have to wait in line.

But she hadn't expected to see Logan Cathcart standing at the counter.

She spotted him through the window as she fed the parking meter. In the past, she probably would have walked on by, and come back for the programs another time. Avoid those butterflies, whenever possible.

But she'd waited too long to find him, to thank him for giving Sean a chance. She pushed open the door. The tinkling sound of the bell caused both Logan and Jasper, who were studying something on the counter, to look up.

"Hi, Jasper," she said. And then there were

the butterflies, right on cue. She took a breath and smiled. "Hi, Logan."

Though Logan smiled back, he looked oddly tense. She advanced toward the counter, telling herself not to take it personally. She didn't know what had put that stiffness in his posture. It might have nothing to do with either her or Sean. Maybe something had gone wrong with his print order.

"You here to proof the programs, Nora?" Jasper, ordinarily the most laid-back of men, looked a bit distracted, too.

"That's okay," she said. "No rush. I can wait until you and Logan are finished."

Jasper shrugged. "We pretty much are finished, I'm afraid. I'm sorry, Logan. I should have called you when Nell's file didn't show up."

The printer looked back at Nora. "Is Nell Bollinger okay, do you know? She was supposed to send over a flyer for Logan's open house, but it never came. I've been trying to call her, but I just get voice mail."

"I haven't talked to Nell in a while," she said. She wasn't surprised, though, that Nell was volunteering for Two Wings. Nell had spent her life working for worthy causes, and even at eighty she wasn't slowing down. "I'll try to find out, if that'll help."

Logan shook his head. "It's no big deal. I'm sure I can patch something together." He patted the countertop. "I'll e-mail you later in the week, Jasper. Good to see you, Nora."

And just like that, he was headed for the door.

She didn't have time to think it through or worry whether she looked a fool. If she was going to talk to him, she was going to have to chase him out onto the sidewalk. And so she did.

He turned when he heard her footsteps behind him. His face was, as always, polite but remote.

"Logan," she said. "I'm sorry to hold you up."

"No problem." He didn't wear a cowboy hat, as so many of Eastcreek's men did. He faced the sun, which turned his eyes the incandescent blue of a butterfly wing. And speaking of butterflies...

She was suddenly trying to swallow past a swarm of them. How did he do that to her? He wasn't flirting, and neither was she. And yet suddenly the air hummed with awareness.

"I wondered if you could tell me how Sean

is doing," she said. "I'm trying to let him handle his responsibility to you on his own, but naturally I'm concerned."

He hesitated only a second or so. And then he shrugged. "He works hard. I can't say he seems thrilled about it, but he does it."

"I'm glad to hear that," she said. "I wondered, because, at home, at least, he's still a little…lukewarm about it."

He chuckled. "He'd have to go a way to reach lukewarm."

"I know." She sighed. "But that first night, when you brought him home, he seemed almost enthusiastic. I was disappointed that his attitude changed so much."

"Me, too." He had his keys in his pocket, and he shifted them, making a jingling sound that hinted he had somewhere to be. "Look, I wouldn't worry too much about it, Nora. He's insecure. I guess that's to be expected."

"But why should he be insecure about working at Two Wings? I saw how you welcomed him. I'd say all of you have been extremely generous and patient, considering the damage he did."

He frowned. He messed with his keys a little more, as if he'd decided to speak his mind.

"Well, I'm not a psychiatrist, but I'd say Sean's having some serious identity problems."

She tilted her head, confused. "What does that mean?"

"I guess it was pretty heady, being Harrison Archer's son. Big man in town. Heir to all he surveyed. But now...now he doesn't really know whether being Harrison Archer's son was a good thing or not. I'd be willing to bet the other kids have said some things."

She thought of Tad Rutherford's shamefaced silence, the day Sean broke the guitar in the music room. Oh, yes, the other kids had undoubtedly been cruel.

"But surely no one there—"

"Of course not. Nobody at Two Wings gives a damn who Sean's father was, or what he did. All we care about is how hard you work, and how much you know about the birds. But Sean's a newbie, and that's how we treat him."

"I see," she said, hearing the ring of truth in his words, and hating it. She wished Logan had known Sean before Harrison's death. Her son hadn't always been like this. Nora had come from a very modest background, and had always worked hard to make sure her boys weren't snobs.

On the surface, anyhow, Logan's assessment

was dead-on. Lately Sean had developed an unbecoming hauteur, and it didn't help that it was clearly feigned. His pride was easily pricked, as if it were no thicker than a soap bubble. He bragged to his friends about how much the new front door cost, the new flowers, the repairs to the fountain, though, ironically, the other children couldn't have been less interested.

He spoke of being *an Archer* in the same tone Evelyn used—a tone that had always made Nora's flesh creep—as if the name itself wore a purple robe and a golden crown.

It wasn't Sean. It wasn't a healthy or helpful reaction to the fear and heartbreak and confusion of this past year.

And it had to stop. Whatever they'd been through, she couldn't coddle him any longer, not to the point that she let this arrogance seep in. Left unchecked, it could permanently stain the fibers of his personality.

She was intensely glad, suddenly, that Sean had been forced into an environment where he was a nobody. Logan Cathcart was an eminently sensible man, with no airs or affectations. A plain *nicer* man, really, than Harrison, for all his good qualities, had ever been.

If Logan would allow Sean to watch him in

action, to make him a role model, it would do her son a world of good.

"Thank you, Logan," she said. She held out her hand.

He hesitated. But then, because it would obviously have been very strange to leave her standing there, on a public sidewalk, with an empty hand outstretched, he took it.

"You're welcome." His hand was warm, his grip firm but neutral. "What for?"

"For everything." She heard the thickness of emotion in her voice. "For not giving up on Sean. For not hating him, even when he's being hateful."

He extricated his hand gracefully, somehow managing not to make it feel like a rejection.

"Let's don't get ahead of ourselves, Nora." His gaze was cool, his smile wry. "I don't want to be a buzz kill, but it's only been a week."

Chapter Five

Two days later, Logan sat in his office, staring at an open e-mail on his computer screen.

It was from Nora. After checking with Nell Bollinger who, it turned out, was quite sick and wouldn't be able to keep her promise to design the open house brochure, Nora had sent over some mock-ups. She'd like to help, she said. He was spending so much time with Sean, the e-mail read. She'd like to even the balance a little bit by helping with the open house. She'd spent years in the PTA doing this kind of thing.

She wasn't bragging. Her sample brochure was good. Clearly she'd already put in a lot of hours. The graphics were interesting, the layout appealing, the text sharp.

Then she'd added a paragraph at the end of the e-mail, casually asking whether he could use any help with the education arm of the sanctuary. She'd always planned to be a teacher, she explained, and she had some ideas that might work.

She listed a couple, as examples. Very intriguing.

Too bad he was going to have to say no thanks. He'd vowed not to let this Sean thing invite all kinds of intimacies that could only lead to trouble. No blurring of the property lines between Bull's Eye and Two Wings, either literally or figuratively.

He hit Reply and then stared at the blinking cursor.

But, vow or no vow, his fingers couldn't find the right words. When you ran a rescue mission like this one, saying no to any help felt insane.

And besides, she was right. He *had* lost valuable hours because of Sean. Not his own hours, of course. He'd kept a safe distance. He wasn't interested in being a surrogate father, and he didn't want anyone getting the wrong idea.

But Matt and Todd, the volunteers he'd assigned to keep an eye on the boy, reported that the kid was a real handful. A constant pain in the butt who thought he was too good for grunt work.

Major flaw. Around Two Wings, ninety percent of everything was grunt-and-sweat work. And with the open house only about four weeks away, Logan needed every available volunteer sweating with enthusiasm. Taking on a brat who needed babysitting had been a really dumb move.

He looked at the attachment again. The brochure she'd designed was perfect. It would save him a fortune in something—either time spent designing one himself, or cash spent at the printer's, having them create something half as nice.

But, open that door a chink...

Crap. He couldn't sit here all day, dithering like a barnyard chicken. He closed the e-mail and decided to decide later.

Right now, his conscience was nagging at him. Maybe his distance from Sean was a bit much. Time to track the kid down and see how he was settling in.

Vic should know. Logan found his manager in the clinic, going through records.

"Let's see… His Highness is *supposed* to be emptying the trash bins," Vic said with a sardonic air that didn't bode well.

"*Supposed* to be?" Logan groaned. "Isn't he *supposed* to be pretty much handcuffed to Todd?"

"Well," his manager said defensively, flipping the binder shut with a bang, "Todd's out sick, and we don't have anyone else available for hand-holding. We're running about a week behind schedule as it is."

Logan cursed under his breath. "Damn it, Vic. The kid's a flight risk, remember? There's not enough insurance in the world to cover our asses if he wanders off."

Vic frowned. "So send him home. I mean it, boss. Get rid of him. We're keeping him away from the birds, but still. He's a disaster waiting to happen."

"Can't," Logan said, hoping he sounded more matter-of-fact than he felt. "But he goes home in half an hour, right? I'll keep an eye on him till five, then I'll send him in to wait for his mom. You'll be here, right?"

"I'll be here till doomsday." Vic pulled another heavy binder from the shelf. "Send him in, and I'll put him to work shredding old files. He'll love that."

Logan shut the clinic door quickly, to keep the air-conditioning in. Wouldn't you know this would be the hottest March in twenty years, when they all had to work like dogs?

Over by the eagle enclosure, he saw three of his volunteers sprawled out in the shade of a hickory tree, shirts off, cheeks pink, water bottles strewn on the grass. Though there were a hundred chores screaming to be handled, he didn't have the heart to complain.

Besides, he needed to find Sean. He wondered how long the kid had been without supervision.

He walked the paths quickly, swinging the lids of the bins as he passed, noting with relief that they all seemed to have fresh, empty bags. Sean must have taken his assignment fairly seriously, and he should be easy to spot, since he'd be dragging around a huge black sack of trash.

Sure enough, Logan found him at the owl enclosure.

The largest of their cages, it was also the most interesting. Shaped like a giant doughnut, with an ancient live oak growing up right through the hole in the middle, the enclosure was shady, mysterious and complicated. Rafters and branches, perches and wooden houses and nesting boxes crisscrossed the area, and the owls themselves were simultaneously everywhere and nowhere. Their strange, noble silence made them initially hard to spot until your eyes learned what to look for.

As predicted, the gigantic, unpleasantly aromatic garbage sack was right behind Sean, deposited on the sidewalk while he pressed himself against the screening, staring into the enclosure.

Logan was pretty sure the boy hadn't heard his approach. Sean's posture, the tension in the fingers pressed against the screening, emanated an intense curiosity that Logan could feel from ten feet away.

"Hey, Sean," Logan said casually. The same tone he might take with an edgy hawk.

Sean twisted his head, and the guilt that moved across his features didn't last long. It was replaced by that characteristic lift of the chin and the steady, impassive gaze that looked remarkably like his father's.

"Did Mr. Downing send you to check up on me? I've been doing the trash. I haven't been goofing off. I just have one bin left."

"Good." Logan didn't follow up on that. Instead he moved inside the rails that had been set to keep the public at a safe distance and joined Sean at the screening. "How's every-body doing in there today?"

"Fine." Sean shrugged. "I guess."

The enclosure was full of owls—a couple of Eastern screech, a pair of barns and at least six barred. "Hard to tell with these guys, isn't it?" Even Logan needed a minute to locate the eerily silent birds, which were lined up, two by two, on the upper rafters. "They're pretty cryptic."

"I don't know what that means." Sean frowned. "Does it mean, like, secretive?"

"Yeah. That's a good word for it. They keep their feelings to themselves. I guess that's why they're so soothing to be around."

Sean nodded absently, as if he had to think about it. "That's true," he agreed, finally. "They're so calm. They let you forget about everything and be calm, too. That's why I like to look at them."

Poor kid. Logan, who sometimes came out here for the very same reason, felt something soften inside him. Behind that steely, arrogant attitude lurked a bewildered kid who was car-rying around memories that would keep most grown-ups awake at night.

But he knew if he made even the slightest sound that hinted at pity, Sean would retreat into his favorite fortress—arrogance. So he just kept watching the owls, who blinked back as if they understood.

After a couple of minutes, Sean turned to look at Logan.

"Mr. Cathcart?"

Logan smiled. "Why don't you call me Logan? Everyone else does."

Sean nodded. "Okay." But he didn't do it. "Mr. Cathcart, I think one of them is sick."

"Sick?"

"Yeah." Sean glanced back into the enclosure. "Maybe."

"Which one?"

"That one on the right, on the first rail up there. He always sits next to the little one."

Logan peered into the shadows. "That's Hamlet. He's an Eastern screech. Why do you think he's sick?"

"I don't know. I watch them every day. He's my favorite. He used to move more. And he isn't very steady, not like the other one. Sometimes I'm afraid he might fall off the rail."

Logan watched the owl carefully. He didn't see anything odd, but he didn't dismiss Sean's gut instinct. He'd seen many trained volunteers spot a tiny alteration in a bird's manner, or eating habits, or mood, and end up saving its life.

If Hamlet did have something…maybe tricho-monas…catching it early would really help.

He made a quick decision. "He might have a parasite. It could give him sores on the roof of his mouth, and he might not be eating enough. Why don't we go get Vic, and see if we can take a look?"

Sean's fingers tightened on the screening. He didn't even turn his head, as if he didn't dare look at Logan and somehow make him change his mind.

"Me?" His voice was small. "You want me to help with the owl?"

"Yeah," Logan said. "If there's something wrong, you're the one who found it. That means you have good instincts." He picked up the garbage sack and slung it over his shoulder. "Come on. Let's get this done before your mom shows up and you have to go home."

But they didn't make it to the clinic. Half-way down the winding path, they met Vic, red-faced and out of breath.

"There's a fire," he said without pream-ble, his voice tight. "Lightning struck a tree over in the woods near Little Creek Estates. Dodie called to warn us. She says we should get ready."

Logan cursed softly. Dodie, the dispatcher

for Eastcreek's fire and police, volunteered at Two Wings every weekend, so she knew what this meant for the sanctuary. Those woods were full of owls, hawks and kestrels. They'd all been run out of their original habitats back in January, when the Little Creek builders had mowed down fifty acres of majestic trees for a tacky new subdivision.

Now fire. Trees downed, nests destroyed. Smoke inhalation, burned wings, orphaned babies. Depending on how fast it spread, the devastation could be terrible.

How many, he wondered, would they be able to save?

Sean touched his arm. "I can stay late, if you want. I can help."

Vic made a noise.

Sean glared at him, then turned back to Logan. "I'll do anything," he said. His eyes were intense, the green flecks burning.

"Okay." Logan put his hands on the boy's shoulders. "But you know what Vic is thinking, right? He's thinking you'll be in the way. We haven't got time to mess with attitude today. If you stay, you have to man up. You get that?"

Sean nodded. "I get it."

"Okay, then, go use the clinic phone to call your mom. Make sure it's okay with her."

Sean was still nodding. He started to run.

"Wait—" Logan made a last-minute decision. He was going to need help worse than ever now. As they said, beggars couldn't be choosers. In his case, beggars couldn't be cowards. "And tell your mom something for me, okay? Tell her I appreciate her offer to help, and the answer is yes."

When Nora entered Jolie's music room, holding Harry by the hand and the spring concert programs under her arm, the place was a mess.

Oblivious to the chaos, Harry ran instantly to the computer, on which Jolie had follow-along music software he loved. He couldn't wait until he was in first grade and had enrichment classes like music regularly on his schedule.

Nora was more in tune with the nuances of the room, and she noticed that Jolie was flushed, uncharacteristically disheveled. She seemed to be emptying her desk drawers into half a dozen cardboard boxes.

"What's going on?" Nora moved one of the boxes an inch to the left, so that she could drop the programs on the desk. She smiled. "If you're quitting because you can't listen to any more of Sean's awful guitar, don't worry. I'm letting him use my old one, and he's promised to practice every day. He should learn that piece any minute."

To her surprise, Jolie didn't laugh. Her face was grim, and she continued to stack sheet music into one of the boxes.

"Not quitting. Never quitting. Can't quit. Some people need their paychecks, remember?" She slammed a book of piano music on top of the stack. "Some people can't afford to swan around donating their time to their favorite charities. Some of us *are* the charities."

Nora felt herself flush as the barb hit home, but mostly she was worried. It wasn't like Jolie to be so spiky. Besides, Jolie knew that Nora would dearly love to be working for a paycheck instead of "swanning" around, trying to find something meaningful to do.

She put out a hand to stop Jolie's fevered stacking. "What's happened?"

The other woman blew strands of damp blond hair out of her face and then squeezed her eyes shut, clearly searching for calm.

"Darn it, Nora, I'm sorry." She dragged the blue band out of her ponytail, scraped the hair into a neat bunch, then wound the band back around it. "It's been a bad day. No. Make that a bad week."

Nora pulled out one of the student chairs and sat down. She didn't have long, because she had to pick Sean up at Two Wings in half an hour. But she'd never seen Jolie look this... disturbed. Not even the day Allison Eckles found a scorpion in her French horn.

She checked to be sure Harry was still tapping the keyboard intently. Then she patted the chair next to her. "Tell me. Maybe I can help."

Jolie laughed without any real mirth, but she took the chair and looked better for it.

"I don't think you can help this time," she said. "This time you're actually the problem."

Nora's eyes widened.

"Well, not you, technically," Jolie amended. "Your sister-in-law."

"Evelyn?"

Jolie lowered her voice, glancing at Harry, though he was obviously in his own world.

"Yeah. Evelyn. She came in last Friday. She wanted to talk to me about Sean. She said she'd heard there'd been an incident with another student in my class, and his guitar ended up broken."

Nora's cheeks felt cold. "How could she possibly know about that? I didn't tell her, and I know you wouldn't. Surely that's not the kind of thing that is discussed outside…"

But then she realized how naive that was.

How had Sean's aunt heard about it? *Ha.* Evelyn Archer Gellner was connected to everyone in Eastcreek. She was a fifth-generation Texan who had married a tenth-generation Texan, and if she wanted to know something, she could always find someone to tell her.

Jeanne Foster, the principal of Eastcreek Elementary, played bridge with Evelyn every Saturday night. Why look any further than that?

"Yeah," Jolie said, folding her arms across her chest. "It sucks, doesn't it? Can't tell you how many privacy laws that violates, but who could prove it?"

"But what did she want from you?"

"She wanted details. She wanted my assessment of Sean's behavior, and his emotional health."

"My God." Nora's hands fisted.

"Right." If possible, Jolie looked even angrier than Nora was beginning to feel.

"What did you tell her?"

"I told her that I was terrifically sorry, but

that simply wouldn't be possible, since she wasn't Sean's custodial guardian. I said that I couldn't, in fact, even confirm that I knew anyone named Sean, and if she needed details perhaps she'd better return to the rumormonger who had told her about it in the first place and request the rest of the dirt."

In spite of herself, Nora laughed out loud. "Oh, good for you, Jolie. I wish I could have seen her face."

"No. Not good for me." Jolie gazed at the chaos around her. "Bad for me. It was gratifying, temporarily. But there's always a price. Ms. Foster informed me yesterday that my music classes will be moved out to the new portable. You know the portable, right? The one with the unit air conditioner that roars but never cools, the floor that creaks and the acoustics from hell?"

"Oh, Jolie." Nora's heart sank. No one could appreciate music in that…dilapidated trailer. She didn't even know what to say. "You think Evelyn…"

Jolie raised her eyebrows. "No one is connecting the dots, you understand, but I'm not a big believer in coincidence."

She stood, picking up another box. "So, if

you really want to help, grab the reeds and mouthpieces out of that cabinet, would you? I've got a lot of packing to do."

Chapter Six

Nora was horrified to hear about the fire. She prayed it would be quickly extinguished, with minimal damage all around. Selfishly, though, she was glad Sean would be staying late at Two Wings today. She didn't want him to get caught in the storm she knew was brewing.

Evelyn was on her way.

Harry was no problem. He was thrilled to hear that he could watch an unexpected hour of cartoons before dinner, and he didn't question his good fortune. An imaginative child, he was already so lost in the giant talking pelican's adventures that he wouldn't notice if Nora and Evelyn started tearing down the rafters.

Nora hoped it wouldn't come to that, but she was certainly mad enough to do some damage.

And Evelyn, who wasn't accustomed to being summoned to Bull's Eye, clearly wasn't exactly feeling sunny, either.

Evelyn had entered moments ago, coming in through the side loggia. She never knocked. It was one of her little gestures that said the house should have been hers, not Nora's. And Nora never asked her to. It was her own gesture, one that said she understood.

Milly ruled the kitchen at this hour, and Harry claimed the family room, so Nora led the way out to the courtyard, where they might get half a chance at privacy. Evelyn didn't sit, though Nora invited her to.

"What is it?" The older woman stood ramrod straight. "You know Ginger is going to drop her litter any day now. I should be there."

"I won't keep you long," Nora said. It showed how upset she was that she had actually forgotten that Evelyn's terrier was about to have puppies. It was the event around which Evelyn's entire life pivoted. "I just thought we should have this conversation face-to-face."

"Is it Sean?" Evelyn tsked, as if she'd expected this. "What has he done now?"

"Sean's fine. It's not about him. It's about Jolie Harper."

The older woman tilted her head. "Who?"

"Jolie Harper." The innocent act didn't fool Nora. "Sean's music teacher."

"Ah." Setting her purse on the bricks, Evelyn arranged herself comfortably on one of the wicker chairs, as if she could relax now that she knew it wasn't anything truly important. "Yes. Miss Harper. Poor woman. She's in a little over her head with that job, isn't she?"

Nora stood behind the lounger, so that she could grip the back. It made a nice shield. "No, as a matter of fact, Jolie isn't over her head. She's one of the most capable, talented teachers I've ever met."

Evelyn lifted one shoulder. "Well, she is a friend of yours, so I suppose you would be defensive of her."

God, Evelyn was an expert at trivializing Nora's opinions. She'd been a little more subtle while Harrison was alive, but since his death she'd pulled out all the stops.

Nora understood that Evelyn's attitude was partly a result of her pain over Harrison's death, which made her more poisonous. Nora could empathize with that.

But she also suspected that Evelyn felt free

to show her true feelings because Nora was boxed in.

Both women knew that the boys needed security. No drama. No big changes. They needed to rebuild their confidence after the horror of this past year.

Evelyn knew that, no matter how unpleasant she was to Nora, shutting her out of the boys' lives was unthinkable. Nora would never make them endure another loss.

"This isn't about friendship, Evelyn. It's about what's fair. And it's not fair for Jolie Harper to be punished just because she wouldn't break the rules to please you."

Evelyn smiled, as if Nora had said something ridiculous. "Punished? That sounds a bit dramatic. If something has happened to Miss Harper, I don't see how that can conceivably be laid at my door."

God, Nora was sick of that supercilious tone.

All of a sudden, she realized that she was very, very tired of being rational. For so long now, she'd tried to be the calm one, the practical one, the one who held everything together after Harrison fell apart.

She had thought she'd done well, but it must have taken a subterranean toll, because suddenly she just wanted to scream.

In the family room, the talking pelican was dancing to "I Believe I Can Fly," the signal that the program was almost over. Somehow, the thought of Harry, cuddled on the sofa with his cartoon-patterned pillow and his muscle-bound action figure, managed to stop her from losing it.

She shut her eyes hard, clamped her teeth together.

"I do lay it at your door, Evelyn. I think you pulled strings to get Jolie banished to a portable classroom, where she will have to work twice as hard to get half the results."

Evelyn laughed. "Good heavens, Nora. I think you overestimate my power. As well as my interest in Miss Harper."

"Maybe." Nora paused. "But perhaps you *underestimate* mine."

Evelyn smiled again. "Fair enough. Still, I'm not sure what was so important that I had to leave Ginger and rush over here. I'd think a simple telephone call would have been adequate if you merely wanted to accuse me of meddling."

This was getting them nowhere. It wouldn't help the boys, and it wouldn't even help Jolie.

"Evelyn, look." In an effort to get past the sniping, Nora kept her voice measured and low.

"If you and I are having problems, shouldn't we try to work them out ourselves? If you want to know something about Sean, don't you think you should ask me?"

Evelyn stood with a snap. Her ramrod posture warned Nora that they'd reached the line in the sand.

"I shouldn't have to ask you," Evelyn said, her eyes narrow and her words sharp. "I shouldn't have to request information from total strangers about the health of my own nephews. Am I not a part of this family? Am I not their blood? The only Archer blood they have left?"

"Evvie, of course you're a part—"

"If Harrison were alive, he wouldn't allow you to exclude me like this. Of course, if Harrison were alive, I wouldn't be so concerned. He knew how to raise an Archer."

Nora lifted her chin. "And I don't?"

"You?" The older woman snorted elegantly. "You haven't got a clue."

After waiting a moment for a response that didn't come, Evelyn picked up her purse and slung it over her shoulder. She headed toward the arched doorway that led to the front yard.

At the last minute, she turned slowly around.

"Let me be very clear," she said. "I don't

give a badger's backside where Jolie Harper teaches her students to plunk the piano. What I do care about is having full access to my nephews. I'd suggest that you inform the school that they're free to talk to me about the boys at any time."

"That sounds like a threat, Evelyn. And if I don't?"

"Miss Harper said she couldn't talk to me because I didn't have any legal rights." Evelyn shook her head slowly. "Isn't that typical? No mention of blood rights, or family rights. Nothing about moral rights. *Legal* rights, that's all they care about. So I was thinking. It might be time for me to look into getting some."

The owlet was going to die.

The vet, Denver Lynch, couldn't tell exactly what was wrong. Well, hell, Logan thought as he washed dirt and soot off his face at the clinic's small sink. What wasn't wrong? The fire had left the little guy homeless, orphaned, scorched, bruised and generally traumatized in just about every way a bird could be.

On the other hand, the tiny, maybe three-week-old barred owl had a brother, also found on the ground by the firefighters, who was probably going to make it.

That was how random life and death were. A split second, a square inch. A literal bolt from the blue.

Mostly, you didn't have any choices, or any real control. You just had to do your best, and if you failed, try to accept it and move on.

Sean Archer, who had been hovering around the clinic for the past half hour as darkness fell, had been asking everyone who emerged how the owl was doing. Clearly he hadn't got the *acceptance* part figured out yet.

It was probably time to send him home. He hadn't been much use since the owlets were delivered.

Unfortunately, while everyone else was busy with a couple of kestrels who had been brought in first, Sean had been the one to accept the basket from the firefighters, and carry it to the clinic door. In that few minutes he'd fallen in love with the downy, helpless creatures with the large, bewildered eyes.

Sean had gone unnoticed for a while in the chaos, staying to watch over the baby birds. When Logan finally noticed him and banished him from the clinic, the boy had been choked with frustration and disappointment. He'd been peeking through the window ever since. Clearly he was deeply invested in the outcome.

"Damn it," Denver said, the sound sudden and heartfelt. "*Damn* it."

Logan glanced over. The look on Denver's face said it all. The little bird's struggle for survival was over.

He ignored the pinch in his chest. You never got over hoping for a miracle, but you knew the odds. "What about the other one?"

Lynch glanced into the cage. "Weak, too, but more of a fighter. We're sure the mother's dead?"

Logan nodded—the firefighters had confirmed it. And their nest, in a hollow of a live oak, had been destroyed completely by the fire. If the owlet lived, they'd have to hope one of the other resident adult owls would "adopt" him.

But that was a big if.

Lynch wiped his face with the back of his hand, then headed over to the sink to clean up. "You going to tell the kid?"

Logan looked out the small window. Sean sat on the steps, chewing on his thumbnail and staring at nothing. He was going to take it hard, and for a minute Logan considered sending someone else to do the dirty work.

But it was just a fleeting cowardice.

"Yeah," he said. "I'll tell him. Want me to

send Matt or Todd in to help feed the survivor?"

"No, he doesn't seem to be hungry. I think I'd wait a couple of hours. For now, just watch."

"Okay." Logan opened the door. "Thanks, Denver," he said.

The words were inadequate, since the vet never took a cent for his work, but Lynch knew they were sincere. "We got lucky tonight, but you know the worst is probably yet to come."

They both knew that most mature, healthy birds were able to fly away from the danger a fire presented. The real crisis hit in the aftermath, when the competition for diminished resources began. Wildlife of all kinds would be wandering the area, hunting for food and shelter. Without their normal habitat, they'd get hit by cars and picked off by predators. They'd need more food to gain sufficient body fat to stay warm, and there would be less to go around.

Two Wings would be inundated. Logan was damn glad he'd sent word to Nora, accepting her help on the brochures. Now if he could just get Sean to calm down and go home, maybe Logan himself could grab a few hours' sleep.

He'd be up all night, watching and feeding the wounded.

The boy whipped his head around as soon as he heard Logan open the door. He was a smart cuss, and he obviously knew how to read faces. He saw the truth on Logan's in the blink of an eye.

"Joe's dead, isn't he?"

Logan nodded. He didn't know the kid had been foolish enough to name them.

"One of them is. The other one is hanging in, so far, at least."

"It's Hank who lived. Even I could tell he was stronger."

"Maybe. But he may not be strong enough. Denver says it's touch and go."

Sean looked furious, and it took Logan a minute to realize he wasn't furious at him, or even at the vet. He was furious at himself for being so weak.

His mouth pressed in on his teeth so tightly it seemed to disappear. His eyebrows dug trenches in his forehead, and his eyes narrowed to hard, glinting slits.

If he could help it, no wussy tear was making it past that blockade.

Logan wasn't a fan of wallowing in emotion, either, but for God's sake, the kid was going to give himself a stroke, holding it in like that. Logan wondered what Sean's dad had said to him about crying. From what Logan had seen of Harrison Archer, he'd guess the man probably mocked emotion as girly and weak.

Or tried to beat it out of the boys, so that they would learn how to be "men."

"I've got to check on the others one more time before we close up," he said. "Want to help?"

Sean didn't respond in words, but he stood, so Logan took that for a yes. He set off down the winding path, stopping at each enclosure and pretending to check on each bird. Max, in particular, was delighted to receive an extra dose of TLC, and hopped over so that he'd be close enough to snag any treats Logan might be bringing.

None of this was strictly necessary, but Logan figured it wouldn't hurt to remind Sean that they logged a lot of successes here, too.

"By the way, Lynch had the chance to check Hamlet out, too. It is trichomonas. Good catch. You may have saved his life."

Sean followed listlessly, obviously not convinced that victory offset the other defeat. When they neared the owl enclosure, he stiffened. He finally met Logan's gaze, for the first time since reading the death on his face.

"What kind of owl was he? He had that funny baby coat, so I couldn't tell."

"A barred owl," Logan said matter-of-factly. He stepped up to the enclosure and peered in. It was almost dark, but just enough light remained to make out the different birds. "There. See the two over on the left? They have big, dark eyes, and a kind of striping, or barring, on their chests."

Sean approached slowly, but then pressed in close and looked in silence for quite a while.

"They're fairly friendly, nonaggressive owls," Logan said. "But they can make quite a racket. When you hear them out in the woods, their hooting can sound downright eerie. They've probably been the inspiration for many a ghost story."

The effort to distract with trivia didn't work this time. Sean didn't even appear to hear him. He seemed intently focused on picking at the wooden brace nearest him.

"How old was he?" Sean didn't look up when he asked. "The baby owl, I mean."

"Between one and two weeks, probably. At two weeks, they lose that pure white downy coat."

Sean's scowl was back, and he dug at the

wood with his finger until Logan worried he might get splinters under his nail.

"Two weeks? That's just a baby," the boy said angrily. "That's so unfair."

Yeah, well, nobody said life was fair, kid. That was Logan's next line in the script, obviously.

But he couldn't bring himself to say it. Sean had already met the injustice of life up close and personal. What he was really asking was *why?* Why wasn't life fair? Why did the good suffer? Why did innocence die?

"I don't know why things like this happen," Logan said. "I don't understand death, and I don't like it. But I'm learning to accept that I can't always stop it."

At that, Sean lifted his head, and the depth of passion Logan saw on those chiseled little features shocked him. The boy was so pale his freckles looked like bruises on a dead man's cheek.

"Accept it?" Sean's voice was reedy, as if his throat were too tight to let normal sound escape. "That's what everybody says. Just accept it, Sean. Get over it. But you don't know what it's like. You don't know one darn thing about it."

They weren't talking about the bird anymore, obviously. Sean glared at Logan as if they were suddenly enemies. His breath wheezed hard and fast, as if he were gearing up for a fight.

Did he want the fight—and the release of tension it might bring?

Or did he want comfort? A gentle word. A hug…

Out of nowhere, like a blow to the rib cage, a memory assaulted Logan. He saw Rebecca bending toward him, her arms outstretched.

And he saw himself, a grown man, just as furious and bewildered as this little boy. Glaring at the one person in the world who actually knew what he was feeling as if she were his enemy. Panting, like a cornered beast.

Turning away from his wife's embrace and any comfort it might bring, fearing he didn't deserve it, knowing it couldn't save him, in the end.

"I do know," he said, though he wasn't sure why. He didn't talk about this. Ever. "I lost someone I love, too. I know exactly how hard it can be."

Sean looked suspicious, unimpressed. "It's not the same. If you lost your dad, I bet he was super old, and my dad wasn't."

Logan almost laughed at the myopic self-absorption of the young. Sean assumed no one on this earth had ever hurt the way he was hurting.

But Logan hadn't lost his father. He'd lost his son. His laughing, bright-eyed, four-year-old little boy, who should have outlived him by decades, who should have gone to college, played football, had children of his own.

He'd watched his son die, that miraculous being that every instinct in Logan's body had been programmed to protect. When Danny took his last breath, the natural cycle of life had split open, and all sense, all meaning, had oozed out.

But Sean didn't know. No one in Eastcreek knew, because Logan had left all that behind in Maine.

And he wasn't going to start jabbering about it now.

It wouldn't help Sean, anyhow. No one ever felt better just because they heard that someone else felt worse.

Grief was an individual sport, and you played only against yourself.

Sean's hands fisted at his sides, needing some recognition that his grief was different. "And I bet your dad didn't go crazy first, so that everyone hated him, and no one will even say his name anymore. It's like he never existed."

Logan's heart squeezed. *Like he never existed...*

"Tragedy makes people uncomfortable," he said. "They're not sure what to say. They're afraid of saying the wrong thing, so they don't say anything at all."

"That's dumb," Sean murmured.

But he didn't sound quite as angry, and Logan wondered whether he'd stumbled on the right tone somehow.

Sean cleared his throat roughly. "My dad was a really good dad."

"I bet he was." Logan could imagine that Harrison Archer could hope for no better epitaph, and he almost said so. He had a feeling the boy wanted to keep talking, and that it might do him good to get some of it off his chest.

But someone else would have to help him with that. Logan had the uncomfortable feeling that he might already have gone too far.

In the enclosure beside them, the barred owl hooted. The melancholy sound echoed into the gloaming around them, and Logan was reminded how late it was.

"I should probably get you home," he said.

"Okay." Sean nodded, and, sure enough, he sounded disappointed.

But he obediently made his way across the mulch, over the barricade and back onto the path. Logan followed. When they reached the bricks, they walked in silence a few minutes, their strides comfortably matched.

"Logan?"

The word caught him by surprise. It was the first time Sean had used it.

"Yeah?"

"I was just wondering. I'm doing this concert thing at school a week from Friday. We're supposed to be selling tickets, to raise money for the band. I'll be playing the guitar. I'm not very good, but—"

He put his hands in his pockets, to show how much he didn't care. "I was wondering if you'd like to buy one."

It took Logan a minute to realize what Sean was asking.

He could have kicked himself into next week. Why hadn't he sent Vic to break the news about the owl? Didn't he know how dangerous it could be, indulging in a heart-to-heart talk about death with a boy as needy as this?

He'd meant to handle it with kindness, but at a professional's distance. He'd meant to treat

Sean the same way he treated all his new volunteers, offering his bracing, sensible philosophy—nothing personal, nothing deep.

But he knew it had gone beyond that. He'd let it get personal.

And now the kid...

Expected something.

Expected Logan to care. Expected him to get involved. To come to his school concert and watch a bunch of kids torture musical instruments for two hours.

Logan's heart rate sped up.

Sean clearly hoped that Logan would want to...to do what Harrison would have done if he were still alive.

To fill the empty seat. And the empty heart, too, perhaps?

But no.

Hell no.

Sean might be looking for a father, but Logan was not looking for a son.

"I don't know," he said, buying time to think of a way out of this. "How much are the tickets?"

"Five dollars," Sean said, still trying to sound completely nonchalant, as if he couldn't care less whether Logan accepted or not. He put a little slouch in his walk, to increase his cool factor, and made a snicking noise with his teeth.

"That seems reasonable." Logan dug in his pocket and pulled out a five. "I can't come to the concert, of course, because you know how busy we're going to be here over the next few days. But I'll be glad to contribute to the cause."

He held out the crisp bill. The silence was so damned awkward Logan felt like smacking something. The kid just stared at him.

It was so uncomfortable he felt the words, "Okay, whatever, I'll come," about to form on his lips.

Then, like salvation, Vic Downing walked by.

"Vic." Logan reached out and grabbed his manager with thinly disguised desperation. "Vic."

The other man stopped, obviously confused. "What?"

"Can you run Sean home, please? He's got school tomorrow, and his mom will be wondering where he is."

Chapter Seven

When Nora heard that Logan had accepted her help with the brochures, she was a little surprised. She'd half expected a polite refusal. He'd already saddled himself with one Archer. She wasn't sure he'd be interested in taking on two.

But she followed up immediately, arriving at Two Wings with a portfolio of ideas before he could change his mind. He thanked her warmly, then assigned his manager, Vic, to oversee her work.

She went over to the sanctuary every day while Sean and Harry were at school. By the end of the week, she was enjoying herself thoroughly, and learning a lot, but she'd seen very little of Logan. She got the distinct impression he was avoiding her.

She had to laugh, wondering if she was, in the end, as big a nuisance as Sean.

But on the rare times Logan came in and listened to her discussions with Vic about new brochures, or scripts for the school education programs, he always seemed impressed at how quickly she was picking things up.

She basked in his approval. And when he told Vic to ask her if she'd like to handle some of the school programs herself, she accepted without hesitation. It was like having one little corner of her dream come true.

She couldn't take on a full-time classroom, not until the boys were older, and the tragedy a more distant memory. But she could still do some good. She could spread the word about the generous work done by everyone at Two Wings.

Somehow, teaching a reverence for life seemed like the best possible antidote for the year she'd just been through.

Late Friday afternoon at the end of her first week, she lingered at her computer in the administration offices. Vic had spent much of the afternoon introducing her to the education birds, ones that were so damaged they'd never be able to live in the wild.

Two Wings had received permits to keep them, as long as they were used regularly to instruct the public about wildlife conservation.

She had fallen absolutely in love with Cadbury, the Harris hawk, a beautiful bird with chocolate brown, black, rust and white coloring. Cadbury had only one wing and a prosthetic beak. His own had been shot off. But he carried himself with the hauteur of a king, and Nora just had to laugh at his wonderful native arrogance.

She had taken a few photos that she hoped she could use in a brochure, and she wanted to play around with them on the computer, seeing how she might design a flyer to hand out at the schools.

She was so absorbed she almost didn't hear the front door open. Since the grand opening was still three weeks away, the ticket office remained locked. But the entrance signage had arrived a couple of days ago, and it occasionally drew in a curious tourist who apparently didn't understand what "Closed" meant.

She glanced up with a smile, reaching for one of the brochures to give as a consolation prize.

But it wasn't a visitor. It was Logan, looking fantastic in jeans and a blue T-shirt the color of his eyes.

"Hi," he said cordially, though he was clearly as surprised to see her as she was to see him. "What are you doing here so late? I thought you picked Sean up at three."

"Not on Fridays," she explained. "He and Harry spend Friday nights with their Aunt Evelyn. They've done it since they were babies."

Another of the rituals she wouldn't dare interrupt, no matter how rocky her relationship with Evelyn was right now. Sean and Harry would think the world had tilted on its axis if they didn't spend Friday nights with Evelyn and her Jack Russell dogs. This week was even more special, because the puppies were due any minute, which would be quite a thrill.

"That's nice." He pulled a blank ledger out of the supply cabinet. "Good that they have family nearby."

She meant to keep her face impassive, but either she wasn't as good at hiding her emotions as she thought, or he was better at reading expressions, because he paused. He watched her a minute, and then he chuckled.

"Not completely good, then? Oh, well. Guess people are the same all over. Believe me, I know all about complicated family relationships."

That was the first piece of personal information she'd ever heard Logan divulge. There'd been plenty of scuttlebutt in town, of course, when he moved in. Maine seemed almost as far away as Mars to native Texans, and they figured it would take something spectacular to drag a Northerner way down here.

The tamest suggestion was that he was divorced and fleeing a broken heart. Others said he was on the lam, one step ahead of the police. One theory was even that he was dying of some dread disease, and had come here to meet his end among the animals.

She didn't believe any of it, and she knew it was unlikely he'd ever volunteer the truth. He had a major case of that WASPy New England reserve.

She hurried to cover her mistake. "Evelyn is a wonderful aunt. She's crazy about the boys, and she'd do anything on earth to help them, if they needed her."

He nodded. "How about you?"

She paused. "I'm not sure what you mean."

"I mean, would she do anything on earth to help you, if you needed her?"

She hesitated a moment too long.

"That's what I thought. Sorry. It's just that I know her, slightly. She's…" He appeared to be searching for a diplomatic word. "Let's just say that two more badly matched people would be hard to imagine. Except—"

Nora felt herself flushing. *Except…*

She knew what he'd been about to say. Except for Nora and Evelyn's brother, Harrison.

"Scratch that," Logan said suddenly, grabbing his ledger and moving toward the door. "I should shut up. It's none of my business."

He was right. She had no obligation to tell him anything about her personal life, and he probably didn't want to hear it, anyhow.

The problem was, she wanted to tell him.

She knew what people had said about her marriage. The whole thing reeked of exploitation. Harrison had been vulnerable after his son's death, they thought. Along came a gold digger who looked a lot like his ex-wife, at least as Peggy had looked in her youth.

Same curly red hair, hazel eyes, petite body.

A woman young and fertile enough to provide the brokenhearted man with a whole new stable of red-haired sons.

For a price.

Mostly, Nora didn't care what anyone

thought. She'd done what she believed to be right, and she had been willing to live with it.

But now, out of nowhere, she wanted Logan Cathcart to understand.

"It's true," she said to his back. "Harrison and I didn't have much in common. Just one thing. One big thing that was more important than all the rest put together."

She took a breath. "I was having his baby."

If this piece of news shocked Logan, the bit of his profile she could see didn't reveal it. He kept his hand on the doorknob, as if he couldn't make up his mind whether he was going to turn it and leave, or let go and listen.

She hoped he would stay. And she thought he might. Her attraction to him, which had been such a shock to her in those early days, hadn't been one-sided. They'd both known it existed, just as they'd both known it could never be pursued.

Even if he no longer felt the chemistry, surely he still felt at least a little curiosity.

"You don't have to explain this to me," he said finally, and his voice was tight. "I don't judge you. I never have."

"I know. But I'd like to tell you, if you don't mind."

He shook his head slowly. "No. I don't mind."

Then he came back into the room, lay the ledger on the table and pulled out a chair.

When he sat, the area felt suddenly intimate. The office, in the center of an empty octagonal building with windows all around, was striped with pale shafts of late-afternoon sun. The trembling shadows of windblown trees moved across the floor. Outside, birds called, unseen, and the crickets had begun tuning up for the sunset show.

"I met Harrison when I was still in college," she said, knowing if she didn't get going she might lose her nerve. "He'd come to South Carolina for a conference, and I was working part-time for the company that catered their meals. He was nice to me, not in the way creepy businessmen sometimes are nice to the hired help. But really nice. He talked to me. He listened."

She waited for a reaction, but apparently Logan was also the type who listened without comment.

She took a breath and went on. "At the time, my mother was very sick. She'd recently lost her job, and she didn't have any health insurance."

For the first time, a flicker of cynicism moved across his features. She didn't blame him. He probably thought she was about to say she'd married the rich older man to pay for her mother's medical care. No one still believed that convenient story.

"Harrison and I got to talking after the dinner. I wondered, at the time, why he seemed so interested in me. It wasn't until we were married, and I met Peggy, that I realized I reminded him of his first wife."

She folded her hands in her lap. "Anyhow, he seemed lonely, and I was in a pretty bad place, too. I told him about my mother. And he offered to loan me the money we needed."

"And you took it."

She lifted her chin. "I took it. There was no question of my refusing it. My mother was going through chemotherapy, and while the doctors and hospitals would do a lot of things as charity, they wouldn't pay for anything they considered a frill. Like the medication that would stop her nausea. Or the stronger painkillers."

His hand moved. "Good God."

"Yes. And there were other things, things that would have made it all so much easier. So when this man offered to help us, with no strings attached, I never even considered getting on my high horse and saying no."

"Of course not," Logan said simply. "I would have done exactly the same."

"Harrison was a good man. He didn't ask for anything in return."

She gave Logan a straight look, to be sure he understood what she meant. "Not anything at all. He just wanted to help. I didn't realize then what he'd been through with Paul, but I think now that it had made him sensitive to suffering."

"Perhaps." Logan's expression remained noncommittal. But then he hadn't really known Harrison before the cancer had twisted him. Before his grief and desire for revenge ate a hole in his heart.

"Anyhow, my mother died a few months later." She blinked and took a second to gather strength for this part. "She had a little life insurance. When I got it, I paid the remaining medical bill, and arranged a very modest funeral. Then I drove to Eastcreek, and showed up at Harrison's door, with the money I owed him in a bag."

Logan smiled. "I'll bet he was surprised to see you."

"He was shocked. But I was shocked, too, because he looked so awful. I told you he'd never asked for anything, and it's true. He never even asked for sympathy. He never told me that his son had recently died in such a terrible way. Ironically, I arrived to pay the money back as the second anniversary of Paul's death was approaching."

Logan had been toying with the ledger on the table, but at that his fingers stilled. "Bad timing," he said neutrally.

"Yes. He was a mess. The house was a mess, too. He'd sent Milly away on an extended vacation. I think it's possible he may have been considering...ending his own life. He didn't ask me to stay, but I did. I cleaned up some of the mess. I cooked him some healthy food. I let him talk about Paul."

"That was very compassionate. Generous, even."

She smiled. "Not really. I didn't have anyone else, and I was used to taking care of my mother. My fiancé—"

Funny that this part should still have any power to hurt. "He had left me while my mother was sick. And while I was at Harrison's house, I learned that Doug had married someone else."

"I'm sorry," Logan said, and he sounded as if he meant it.

"It's okay." She hadn't thought about Doug

in years, but now she could remember that night so clearly. She hadn't wanted her faithless fiancé back, but hearing that he was married…that the door was forever closed…

After her mother, the sense of loss was dreadful.

Logan shifted in his seat.

She knew he was uncomfortable, because she'd reached the heart of the story. "I'm sure you can see where this goes. Two lonely, hurting people, in the same empty house…"

He nodded.

"Right. My last night there, Harrison asked for comfort, and I gave it to him. He was a kind man, a good man, but so lonely. I knew I could make some of his pain go away. What would it cost me to give him one night?"

"A lot, apparently," Logan observed softly. "Ten years of your life."

"In a way, that's true. But in another way—" She swallowed hard. "Two months later, I discovered I was pregnant. I considered having the baby alone. I didn't love Harrison Archer, and he didn't love me. We didn't have to try to make a family just because of one mistake. I had plans for my life, and they didn't involve moving to Texas and being the wife of a man twice my age. I told myself he would never know."

"And yet…" Logan's eyes were gentle. "Apparently you changed your mind."

"In the end, I couldn't be that selfish."

To her horror, her voice had begun to sound raw, scoured with emotion. It was painful to think back on that moment. So many people believed she'd come rushing back, thrilled to stake her claim to the Archer fortune, but it had felt like reporting for a firing squad.

"I was carrying the child of a man who had already lost one. How, after what he'd suffered, could I deny him the new hope a new son might bring? So I came back to Eastcreek, back to Bull's Eye, and I told him about the baby."

"But surely…you didn't have to marry him, just because there was a baby on the way. People often—"

"Not Harrison. He had very strong ideas about family. About Bull's Eye, and Texas and the Archer name. I knew he would want the real thing. And whatever anyone, including Evelyn, might think, I was a good wife to him. I gave him sons, and I gave him a happy home."

She wished she didn't sound so defensive. She wasn't talking to Evelyn now. And Logan had never so much as hinted that he disapproved of her.

Besides, surely Harry was proof that she'd been fair to Harrison. She'd really, really tried to love him with all her heart. She'd admired him, and she'd pitied him, and she'd cared deeply for his well-being. That was pretty close to love, wasn't it?

Eventually they'd conceived Harry. After that, as if Harrison really had just wanted an heir and a spare, he rarely came to her room. Their marriage settled into a loyal, platonic partnership, and she couldn't deny it was a relief.

But she was still young, and coming into her prime as Harrison was emotionally and physically withdrawing from her.

Surely that accounted for the rogue sparks when she met Logan. As unfulfilled as she was, how could she have stopped herself from responding to the virility and charm of the new young neighbor who was so gentle with the wounded birds who found themselves in his hands?

She never once sinned with her body, not even by the lightest brush of a finger. But with her mind...

She tried to smile at him now.

"So. That's the whole strange story."

His fingers had returned to toying with the ledger, but he watched her with shadowed eyes. "Does Evelyn know all this?"

She nodded. "She doesn't believe it, of course. She always thought I was just after the money, and when Harrison left Bull's Eye to me, she was sure of it."

"But you're obviously essentially a custodian. You aren't going to sell it, or mortgage it for furs and trips to Paris. Any fool can see that you're holding on to it for the boys. And Harrison knew he could trust you to do exactly that."

"Yes. That's all true. But for Evelyn, the very fact that my name...that I have control... She doesn't understand."

One side of Logan's mouth went up, but Nora couldn't quite call it a smile. "It makes perfect sense to me," he said, "and I'll be glad to explain it to Evelyn, if you'd like."

She laughed. "Oh, Lord, no. Please don't tell her I talked to you about this. She already—"

He lifted one eyebrow and waited.

She faltered. "Well, she already thinks Sean and I spend too much time over here."

He stood, as if that was the cue he'd been waiting for. "Then you'd better get home," he said. "Because whatever Ms. Evelyn Archer is thinking, I definitely want to prove her wrong."

Nora couldn't tell how Sean felt about her involvement at the sanctuary. His attitude toward Two Wings, and toward Logan, in particular, seemed to seesaw dramatically.

The psychiatrist, with whom Sean's weekly visits had resumed, assured Nora the mood swings were normal, but they troubled her anyhow.

Some days, Sean seemed to adore his sanctuary work. One afternoon, when she'd taken the boys to the library, he'd checked out an armload of books about birds. That night, she'd heard him reading a description of the American bald eagle to Harry as a bedtime story.

But other days, he returned home sullen and uncommunicative.

Today, a week after her talk with Logan in the Two Wings office, Sean had come home in such foul humor that she'd been afraid something had happened to the owlet they'd rescued from the fire.

Sean had clearly adopted that bird emotionally. His name was Hank, apparently, and he updated her on Hank's progress every day. She lived in fear of the bird succumbing to some delayed reaction to his trauma.

But today, when she asked him if everything was okay at the sanctuary, he had grumbled, "I just can't stand Mr. Cathcart. He thinks he knows everything, but he doesn't."

She'd been afraid Sean might go into such a serious sulk that he'd refuse to perform in tonight's school concert. He'd been up and down about that all week, too.

Sometimes he would practice for an hour straight to get one arpeggio right in his intro to "The Star Spangled Banner."

Other times, he'd refuse to touch the instrument. The concert, he'd insist, was "majorly lame."

But when Jolie arrived to take him over to the auditorium to help her set up, he was ready to go. He'd even packed his suitcase and left it by the front door. Since it was Friday, he and Harry would be going home from the concert with Evelyn.

After Sean left, Nora helped Harry pick out his nice clothes. As she rummaged through his drawer for matching socks, she asked him whether he thought his kindergarten class might like to see a Two Wings program about the birds.

Harry scoffed, sounding just like his brother.

"Not if Mr. Cathcart does it," Harry said, ducking his chin as he shoved his shirttails into his pants. "He's a jerk. He probably wouldn't come anyhow. He's not coming to Sean's concert."

Nora laughed. "Why would Mr. Cathcart come to Sean's concert? He's far too busy for that."

"He's not too busy. He just doesn't like kids."

Nora, who had watched Logan with his teenage volunteers, knew that was far from true. Sean was obviously the source of this pronouncement, and she wondered why he would tell Harry such a fib.

"Really?" She held out two black socks triumphantly. "What makes you think he doesn't like kids?"

"Well, he doesn't like Sean, anyhow. He said he won't come tonight, even though he has a ticket. Sean gave him one."

Oh... Nora bit her lower lip, suddenly seeing the light.

Sean had asked Logan to attend his concert.

She could hardly imagine her thorny, defensive son taking such a risk. He rarely admitted to wanting anything these days, for fear he wouldn't get it. He couldn't stand being pitied, or looking weak.

And he absolutely never put himself in the position to chance being rejected.

Yet he'd invited Logan to his concert.

And Logan had turned him down.

No wonder Sean had been so glum as he got ready tonight. Nora had thought his snarly attitude was a reaction to the extra work of having to set up the equipment for Jolie. She hadn't felt much sympathy.

Now she saw something much more poignant. This was the first school function he'd participated in since Harrison's death. He would be the only member of the band without a daddy in the audience.

Oh, if only Sean had mentioned his plan to Nora. She could have warned him that Logan was not the kind of man who rushed into intimacy. She could have explained Logan's obligation to keep a professional distance from his employees, volunteer or otherwise.

She might even have found some other male friend who might be willing to represent Sean in the audience. Denver Lynch, the vet, maybe. She'd known Denver for years, and they were friendly enough that she could have asked a favor.

But Sean hadn't told her. And she hadn't guessed.

So all she could do now was put the best possible face on the situation.

"He said he couldn't come? Well, that's Mr. Cathcart's loss, then," she said brightly, "because it's going to be a wonderful concert, isn't it?"

Harry smiled. He might try to copy his big brother's cool sneer, but his natural state would always be sunny.

"Yep," he agreed as he worked to tie the bows on his dress shoes. "I'm going to play in concerts when I'm in fourth grade, too."

She hustled him out the door with an eye on the clock. In spite of a fierce thunderstorm that slowed traffic, they arrived in plenty of time. The auditorium was already crowded.

Jolie clearly knew that a big cast of performers was the secret to an impressive turnout. Every singer had a solo, even if it was only a few words, and every musician had a moment in the spotlight, too. Sean's would be the short but fancy intro to the national anthem.

Evelyn had arrived first, probably trying to beat the rain, and had saved seats in the front row.

Darn it. Nora had hoped for something a

little farther back. Evelyn's judgmental gaze wouldn't make it any easier for Sean to pull off that arpeggio that had been giving him so much trouble.

But she had no option. She led a damp and tousled Harry to the seats, put him in the middle, and gave Evelyn a perfunctory kiss on the cheek. The gesture was mostly for show, since many of Evelyn's friends were here, and she would have accused Nora of embarrassing her publicly if the greeting had been cool.

They hadn't made peace yet, and Nora didn't see a real truce being likely as long as Evelyn's threat about getting "legal rights" hung over their heads.

Nora didn't honestly believe any judge would dream of taking these boys away from their mother, not after they'd already lost their father.

Still. It made her nervous.

She waved at Tad Rutherford's mother, a very sweet woman who had been bending over backward to be friendly ever since the incident in the music room.

Then she glanced through the program, though she knew it by heart, having put it together herself.

Anything to keep from making small talk with Evelyn.

She needn't have worried. The other woman was absorbed in Harry, retying his shoelace and straightening his collar. When she began brushing his wet bangs out of his forehead, he started to wriggle.

Nora realized she'd have to provide a distraction.

"Did you see Sean?" She caught her sister-in-law's gaze. "He's wearing the jacket you bought him last week. He loves it."

Evelyn offered her a chilly smile, but she didn't stop adjusting Harry's hair. She hated the boys' cowlicks, and was always working to subdue them.

"No, I haven't seen him. He's backstage, I assume, and busy."

Harry began to lean toward Nora, trying to get away from his aunt's hands. That would hurt Evelyn's feelings, so Nora wracked her brain for something else to say.

"Evelyn, I was wondering if—"

But something over Nora's shoulder had caught Evelyn's attention. Her black eyes sharpened.

Whatever it was, Evelyn didn't like it.

Nora swiveled, looking behind her. She hoped to God Sean hadn't taken off the jacket.

Evelyn grasped Nora's shoulder with her cold fingers. She leaned close, over Harry's head, and spoke in a low, severe whisper.

"Did you invite him?"

Who? Nora scanned the crowd, which was overflowing now. The student ushers were leading newcomers to standing-room-only positions along the wall.

Then she saw him.

Logan.

He had come after all.

In spite of Evelyn's obvious enmity, her heart lifted. For Sean's sake, of course. She was happy, because now Sean would have no reason to feel rejected.

Their eyes met, and after a couple of seconds Logan smiled. He shrugged slightly, as if to say his presence was something of a surprise to him, as well.

Evelyn's fingers tightened on Nora's shoulder. "I said, did you invite him?"

"No," Nora answered calmly. She glanced at Evelyn's hand, and the older woman removed it. "No, I didn't."

"Sean did," Harry said. He knelt on the chair

to get a better look. "But we thought he wasn't going to come. He hates kids."

The students began filing onto the stage and arranging themselves in their positions. The principal musicians on chairs, the chorus on small risers, the MCs at the mics.

Nora found Sean, ready to give him the thumbs-up that had always been their special signal.

He wasn't looking at his mother, though. He was studying the audience, just as she had a minute ago. His eyes were dark, mutely hungry, darting from face to face, searching for the one he was afraid he wouldn't see.

He had set his jaw so that neither relief nor disappointment could show in his mouth.

But there was nothing he could do about those eyes.

When he spotted Logan, everything changed.

He didn't smile. He didn't move a muscle. But a spark instantly lit the darkness of his gaze.

Nora doubted whether anyone, even Logan himself, or Evelyn with her eagle eyes, would notice it. If Nora didn't know Sean to the core, even she might have missed the little flare of pleasure.

But she saw it. And, paradoxically, the warmth of that spark sent a chill through her veins.

Because there was no answering spark in Logan's eyes. He had come here to be polite, nothing more. She glanced at her son, who was so confused and lonely, and who obviously had pinned so many secret hopes on this kind, interesting, slightly remote neighbor.

A man who was, in spite of the accidental proximity of their homes, essentially a stranger.

She'd have to talk to Sean. A gentle warning. Go slowly. Don't invest too much too soon...

She couldn't stop herself from looking around one more time. Logan's gaze was on her still. She flushed like a teenager and turned back, praying that Evelyn hadn't noticed.

But as the lights dimmed, and Sean's opening notes floated out into the hushed auditorium, Nora wondered...

Go slowly...

Was she talking to Sean? Or was she talking to herself?

Chapter Eight

It was going to rain again, and if Logan wanted to get the roof of the hawk enclosure patched, he didn't have much time. He'd been a fool to waste two hours going to the elementary school concert.

A royal fool. In so many ways.

But it was done. It couldn't be undone, and he wasn't going to waste any more time regretting it. When the curtain came down, he hustled out of there, deftly avoiding getting entangled in any chitchat with the friendly Eastcreek PTA, especially Nora or Evelyn.

When he got home, he quickly stripped off his button-down shirt and khakis, switching to a pair of filthy jeans and a sweatshirt with more holes than fabric. It was a relief to be home again. He should just accept that he was more comfortable with the birds, who didn't want anything from him except food and medicine.

If only everyone else would accept that, too. Maybe, he thought with a chuckle, he should get a baseball cap that said Hermit: Approach with Caution.

Then the doorbell rang.

He should ignore it. He was cranky, and he didn't feel like making small talk, especially not if it turned out to be Annie. Logan had made the mistake of asking her out a second time last week, and then, over dinner, committed the cardinal sin of admitting he hated to cook.

He might as well have painted a target on his back.

Since then, Annie had shown up at the cabin every other night, with a casserole or a plate of brownies in her hands. The gesture was so nice—hell, *Annie* was so nice—that he knew he should invite her in. But he couldn't raise hopes he had no intention of fulfilling. So he'd walk her to her car, trying not to feel like a jerk who'd just kicked a kitten to the curb.

Lord, don't let it be Annie, he thought as he shoved his feet into his sneakers without even untying them.

"I'm coming," he called out as the doorbell rang again.

He opened the door.

Aw, hell. Take that back…he'd rather deal with Annie any day.

It was Nora. And instead of an armful of cookies, she held an armful of papers.

"Hi," she said softly. "I have the flyers for the school programs. I thought you might like to see them."

It was just an excuse, really, and they both knew it.

In a way, a lot like Annie. And yet, completely different.

By all normal yardsticks, he should have found it even easier to send Nora away. She had none of Annie's assiduously cultivated sexuality. Nora looked as skinny and small as a kid, and the cloudy night snuffed out the fire of her hair. She still wore her swingy green dress from the concert, but it looked a little big for her, as if she'd recently lost weight. The yellow bug light on his porch turned her complicated hazel eyes gray.

And yet…

He should say something. She looked uncomfortable. But what?

I'm one mixed-up son of a bitch, and I don't feel like talking, and I damn sure don't want to be your kids' new daddy, but I sure would love to have sex with you right now.

"Did I come at a bad time?" She cleared her throat and shifted her weight to her other foot. "It's not just the flyers, really. I also wanted to thank you for coming to Sean's concert tonight. It meant a lot to him."

"No problem." Hell, he even sounded like a hermit. A cave dweller. Grouchy, husky, unaware of basic social refinement. "Look, Nora, about tonight."

She blinked, and he thought maybe her fingers tightened on the stack of flyers.

"About tonight," he began again.

He couldn't decide how to finish the sentence. He had started out thinking he'd say something about Sean, and how the kid probably should stop coming here before he got too attached.

Then he thought, forget Sean, the important thing is to make her go home.

But then he tried to imagine her walking away, setting the flyers down and getting back into her car. He tried to imagine her driving away, and the relief he'd feel once she left.

Except that he didn't feel relieved. He felt… alone.

He might not want to be with Sean. Or the Eastcreek PTA. Or Annie with the brownies.

But he did want to be with Nora. His subconscious, that sneaky, self-absorbed manipulator, had already done the calculations. It was Friday. The boys would be with their aunt. She wouldn't have to rush away.

For a little while, she could forget, maybe, that she was a mother, or a widow, or anything but a woman.

Perhaps she could even make him forget.

"What about tonight, Logan?" She frowned slightly, as if something in his manner had begun to worry her. "Is everything okay?"

"Yeah. It's fine." He set his shoulders and took the leap. "It's actually lucky that you stopped by. I have to patch the roof of the hawk enclosure, which means getting up on the extension ladder. Any chance you'd be willing to hold it steady for me?"

She smiled, reassured.

"I'd be honored," she said, and the small musical note of laughter in her voice went right through him.

He took the flyers, dropped them on the hall table, then led her around the side yard, toward the sanctuary. It would have been quicker to go through the house and out the back, but he didn't trust himself that close to the bedroom.

At least out here the owls were always watching.

It was a long walk through winding paths lit only by the moon and a series of small, glowing landscape globes. Hoping to avoid a discussion of Sean, he opened a conversation about his great-aunt Doreen, who had left this land to him. Nora had known Doreen better than Logan had, having been her next door neighbor for ten years.

The old lady had been the black sheep of the Cathcart family, an elderly flower child who lived in a little log-and-stone house and grew her own food. Growing steadily more eccentric, she never made it to Maine, and the mainstream Cathcarts rarely came here to visit her.

"She was a real pistol," Nora said, laughing. "She drove Harrison crazy, of course, because he wanted to buy her land, and she wasn't one bit interested, no matter how much he offered. Finally she told him if he didn't stop badgering her, she'd get a restraining order."

Logan laughed. He'd never heard that story.

"I only met her once," he said. "I was about Sean's age. The family went on a driving vacation that summer, and we ended up here for a few days. My parents were shocked. They laughed about the visit all the way to the Grand Canyon, but I loved being with Doreen. I loved her weird meals, which actually tasted fantastic. I was sure she could talk to the animals, and I wanted to learn how she did it."

Nora smiled. "Is that why she left the land to you? Did she know you were going to take up rehabbing?"

"God, no. No one knew, not even me." He thought about his mother's appalled face when she heard. "I'm the first Cathcart since...since the Mayflower, probably...not to practice law."

He was watching the muddy path, but he could feel the pause in her step as she turned to look at him.

"Why didn't you follow the family tradition?"

"Actually, I did. For about three years. It wasn't for me."

Simple, but essentially true. No need to go into all the reasons why he'd needed a change. No need to mention Rebecca, or Benjamin.

Or Danny.

She touched his arm lightly. Too lightly to

account for the sizzle that sped through his veins.

"Well," she said. "I know a bunch of wounded birds who are very glad you decided not to stay a lawyer. And a lot of people, too."

He didn't answer her. He didn't dare. God only knew what he might have said. Or done. Just walking along beside her, keeping a respectable distance, talking about casual things—and he couldn't stop thinking about sex.

The wind blew her skirt against her thighs, and his groin tightened. The air carried her perfume to his nose, along with the musky scent of the approaching storm, and he started to burn in all the wrong places.

He should have sent her packing, just like Annie. Only faster.

Finally, after an aeon of that torture, they reached the birds. He grabbed a couple of flashlights from one of the equipment sheds and handed one to her. The landscape lights were kept dim, so that they wouldn't bother the birds, and the moon kept skimming in and out of rainclouds, so it wasn't much use.

Then he switched on a spotlight he'd put out earlier, which shone directly on the damage he'd have to repair.

"Oh, no." Nora spotted the mess at the hawk enclosure immediately. The thunderstorm this afternoon had brought a lot of wind. One of the old oaks had lost a branch that drove straight through the roof of the hawk enclosure, like a spear.

"Is Max all right?"

"He's fine. He was hunkered down at the back, trying to stay dry, like the pampered princess he is. But that branch leads dangerously close to the torn spot. If he took a notion to go wandering, he could probably get out."

Logan pulled out the big blue plastic tarp he'd left beside the enclosure. He'd considered skipping the concert to fix the roof right away, but at the last minute decided Sean needed him more.

Logan had been gambling on Max's laziness to keep him inside, and he was relieved to see he'd won that bet.

The hawk was still standing where Logan had seen him last, on the back perch, with his baby toys scattered on the sand of the cage floor around him, gleaming wetly. Max was nearly domesticated in some ways. He loved toys almost as much as he loved treats.

Logan held out the tarp. "Tonight, I just need

to attach this up there. Vic will arrange a permanent repair tomorrow."

"Can I hand it up to you? It looks pretty heavy."

"I've got it." He set the ladder in place. "But if you'd pass me the hammer and those nails when I'm ready, that would be a big help."

She nodded, and he began to climb. She obediently put her hand on the edge of the ladder and watched him ascend. He glanced down at her once, and couldn't help smiling at her serious expression.

Apparently she didn't know what a crock this "ladder holding" job really was. Or maybe she didn't care. She clearly was just glad to be a part of it all.

She'd been comfortable at the sanctuary from the get-go. Logan had trained a lot of volunteers in the past eighteen months, and he knew a natural when he saw one. Even the birds sensed it and were less agitated when she entered their cages to help with feeding or cleaning.

Sean was different. Even though he obviously had good instincts—his gut feeling that Hamlet was sick had probably saved the owl's life—he still upset the birds whenever he came near. Maybe the creatures recognized Texas hunter-rancher DNA when they smelled it, or maybe his inner turmoil simply emitted bad vibes.

Vic wouldn't let Sean do any feeding, grooming...anything that brought him too close to the birds.

Logan spread out the tarp along the roof. Luckily, the branch had gone all the way through, so he didn't have to get out the chain saw and free the screen.

As he unfolded the blue plastic, Max let out a scratchy caw. But Logan could hear that the hawk wasn't annoyed. Just talking to Nora, probably, urging her to notice him.

She handed up the tools, and their fingers collided clumsily. For a minute he was glad she was holding the ladder, because he definitely wasn't as steady as he ought to be.

Back to work, damn it. Trying not to hammer so hard he woke up every bird in the place, Logan set a nail as an anchor. He tied the tarp to the nail with the twine that wound through the eyelets.

He set his best knot in the twine, then used shorter lengths to tie the tarp to the mesh. Finally he leaned back to survey his work.

It wouldn't survive a hurricane, but it probably would last the night.

"Okay, coming down," he warned Nora, as he stepped backward down the ladder. He was careful. The ground was muddy, which made his sneakers slick, and the rungs were slippery, too.

The last thing he wanted was to pitch off this damn thing and crush her beneath him.

Right?

He made it down. But she was still right there, hanging on to the wet silver leg of the ladder, not sure when it was all right to let go.

He smiled to show he was in one piece, and she smiled back. As their gazes locked, the moment hummed with awareness. They were alone, except for the birds.

"Logan," she said, her voice stilted. "I really did want to thank you for tonight. I know you didn't have the time to spare, but it meant a lot to Sean."

He wasn't breathing quite right. The nearness of this woman seemed to do something to the air.

"It was nothing," he said, equally stiff.

"Not to Sean, it wasn't. I don't know if you saw his face, but—"

"I saw it." He fought to keep his voice even. "And you know what it told me? It told me I shouldn't have gone there in the first place."

"But—"

"Listen to me, Nora. I feel sorry for him. I do."

That was why, in the end, he'd decided to go to the concert. He knew how hard it had been for Sean to admit that he wanted anything, that he cared whether anyone came to see him play the guitar or not. Logan understood that kind of pride. He knew how humiliating it would be to ask, and be rejected.

"But the truth is, I can't take him on. I'm not interested in taking anyone on. Not in that way. Do you understand?"

She nodded awkwardly, and he knew she had understood that he meant her, too. He wasn't looking for any permanent commitments.

He wondered if he'd hurt her. But damn it, it was true, and if they were going to do anything dumb tonight, he didn't want to do it under false pretenses.

"Yes, of course I understand." Her eyes were wide and liquid in the cloudy moonlight. "It'll be all right. I'll talk to Sean. I'll make sure he understands, too."

But Sean wouldn't understand. Logan knew he'd made a mess of it, and it would be desperately difficult to untangle things now. He'd failed to draw the proper boundaries, and now they'd reached that unhappy fork in the road.

Sean would either go forward in intimacy, ready to care about Logan and let him into his life, or he would go forward in deep resentment and anger, with a hatred born of imagined rejection.

Finding a middle road would be so delicate…

Almost as impossible as finding that same middle road with Nora. They, too, stood at a forked path.

He knew he should step back. This attraction, as intense as it was, couldn't lead to anything but a few hours of pleasure, followed by awkward regret.

He knew the Nora Archers of the world. He knew what they needed from a man.

And what she needed, he no longer had to give.

And yet he *was* still a man.

A man who was burning up with sexual frustration, standing here in the glare of the spotlight, with wet darkness all around him. Standing so close to this pale, worried mom who should have been off-limits.

Behind them, the trees and shrubs were shifting, whispering, rustling with anxiety about the storm that was headed their way. Even the birds had begun to fidget and call, and lift their wings in fear.

He hadn't felt this kind of lust in…in years. He wasn't sure he'd ever felt it, not quite like this. It was simultaneously exciting and painful. Strangely helpless and yet thrillingly alive.

In the end, he simply didn't have the self-control to stop himself.

He lowered his head, till he was no more than a feather's distance from her lips. He paused there, just long enough for the word *no* to be spoken. But it didn't come. Instead, he felt the warmth of her breath like small, eager waves against his mouth, coming faster, faster…

The feeble protests of his conscience never had a chance.

Her half-parted mouth was sweet and hot, and the instant he touched it, he needed more. As he drove deeper, he sensed a strange uncertainty in her touch, some complex kind of confusion. But it didn't mean *no*. Her hands pressed themselves against his chest, and they were kneading softly, an age-old gesture he recognized well.

Oh, he'd missed this…he'd missed this so much. There was such blissful relief in this, losing yourself in another person, letting passion burn away your thoughts until your mind was a clean, white slate.

He welcomed the fire. He moved hard across the satin heat of her lips, and claimed the inner darkness, too. He inhaled the perfume of wildflowers and rain that belonged uniquely to her. He blindly registered, with pulsing heat and a delicious, focused pain, the contours of her body, her breasts against him, her hips under his hands....

He lowered his head, and let his kisses trail along her neck, her shoulder. Her collarbone, as fragile as a starling, and then the gentle swell beneath. He bent further, his lips seeking, his hands moving over the buttons of her dress.

And then, just as he lay the silky green fabric aside, and bared the glowing white lace of her bra, the milky curve of her breast, Max began to scream.

The screeching, air-splitting sound made even Logan's hair stand on end. He could only imagine how it frightened Nora. She gasped, whipping her head toward the sound, and jerked away.

In the bushes, something rustled heavily, as if it, too, had been panicked by the sound. Nora stared at the shivering foliage, her lips parted, her hands holding the edges of her open bodice.

Within seconds, the bushes nearest Max's enclosure fell silent. But a few yards away, just beyond the reach of the sanctuary lights, other bushes cracked and shifted. As they stood there, the sounds moved even deeper into the trees, gradually growing more muted, waning yard by yard.

Then they were gone.

"Nora," he said. He touched her elbow. "It was nothing. It was probably a raccoon."

He meant it. It could have been a possum, a boar or a large stray dog. Max didn't like large animals. "It could have been anything."

She held her shirt together with pale fingers as she stared off into the murky forest, and he knew she was trying to read the darkness.

"It was nothing," he said.

She turned, finally, and looked at him. Her eyes were no longer frightened. But their expression was bleak, and he knew that, over the course of one small minute, everything had changed.

"Nora," he said. "It wasn't Sean."

She glanced once more into the trees, and then she looked at him and nodded.

"I know," she said. Her voice was ragged, as if she still hadn't caught her breath. "But... it could have been. And that's all that really matters."

He tried not to argue, though his body was aching with frustration. It could have been Sean. Evelyn's house was only a mile or two away. She might believe she was the perfect guardian, but a smart, determined kid could outwit her if he was determined enough.

Logan and Nora both knew Sean had already run away twice, and both times he'd come to Two Wings.

Yes. Though they knew it wasn't Sean, they also knew it *could have been.*

But was that really the *only* thing that mattered?

Suddenly Logan understood why he'd felt confusion in her kiss. She hadn't been confused about her own desires. She wanted him as much as he wanted her. But she had been confused about Sean, and what this might mean for him.

Obviously, since Max's cruelly timed wake-up call, she wasn't confused anymore.

Most normal nine-year-old boys could handle the sight of their mom kissing a new man.

But Sean wasn't a normal boy.

Her blouse was almost rebuttoned now. She was going home. Or perhaps to Evelyn's house, to satisfy her maternal fears and see her son sleeping in his bed with her own eyes.

"Come on," he said, accepting defeat, and trying to remember that it was probably for the best. "I'll walk you to your car."

Nora called Evelyn from her cell the minute she got on the road.

She knew it hadn't been Sean in the bushes. It couldn't have been.

But if it *had* been, where would that leave him now? Alone in the middle of nowhere, in the middle of the night? Hiding somewhere in the empty acres beyond the sanctuary lights?

She had to know.

"Nora? What's wrong?"

Evelyn had caller ID, and she somehow thought it exempted her from the need to answer the phone normally.

"Hi, Evelyn," Nora said, straining to hit her standard tone. Her guilty conscience made her think that her lips sounded thick, as if they'd just been roughly kissed. "I just wondered if Sean was still awake."

"No, he's sleeping, of course. You know

I enforce a very strict bedtime when they're here."

Yes, yes, Evelyn did everything exactly right. Nora didn't give a damn about that power struggle now.

"I'm sorry to ask, but can you put him on the phone, anyway? I—"

I...what?

Nora's mind was still slightly dazed, and she wasn't mentally sharp enough to think of a good excuse. The dark road slid beneath her tires, and she had to work to remember where her turns would be.

"I promised him I'd call and say good-night. Please, Evelyn, put him on the phone."

"No. That's absurd." Evelyn sounded prim but not displeased, as if she enjoyed being able to deny Nora anything. "He didn't say a word about hearing from you. He's asleep."

"I know." A weakness suddenly assaulted her. Perhaps it was the ebbing of the adrenaline, leaving her drained and hollow. She fought it. "Evelyn. Just wake him up. Please."

The older woman hesitated. "What's the matter with you, Nora?" Her voice was suspicious. "Are you even at home? Have you been drinking?"

Finally, Nora lost her patience. Who did this woman think she was, keeping Nora from her son?

With shaking hands, she pulled to the side of the road and stopped the car. Rain had begun to splatter against the windshield, and she needed to concentrate.

"You know I don't drink, Evelyn. Put Sean on the telephone, or I'll come by there and wake him up myself. If I have to do that, I warn you this will be the last time he ever spends the night at your house."

Even through the airwaves, Nora could feel the other woman's outrage. The only response was the sound of Evelyn's breathing, slightly more labored as she climbed the stairs to the side-by-side rooms where Harry and Sean slept when they visited.

A door creaked, followed by a muffled whisper.

And then, thank God, the sound of her son's sleepy, worried voice.

"Mom? What's up? Is everything okay?"

She gripped the phone so hard her fingers hurt. She shut her eyes and let her head fall against the headrest.

"Everything is fine, honey. Everything is absolutely fine."

Chapter Nine

Maybe, Logan told himself in the frustrated days after the kiss, it had been all for the best.

Maybe, in the end, it would actually make things easier.

Maybe, instead of complicating things, the kiss would clear the air. The chemistry between them had always lurked invisibly in the undercurrents. Sparks flew, tension built…but it was all too shameful and dangerous to speak of.

Would they? Wouldn't they?
Should they? Shouldn't they?
The questions had been driving them both insane.

Now they'd hauled it out in the open. They'd looked it straight in the eye, named it and discovered that they did, ultimately, have the power to resist it.

He knew it wouldn't completely eliminate the electricity, or the energy that fizzed between them if their shoulders or fingers accidentally touched. But surely it would help. Now they knew where they stood. He'd been honest about what kind of relationship he offered. She'd turned it down.

The decision was made. They would be friends only.

Working together should be pretty simple from here on out.

If she came back at all, that was.

She wasn't expected until today—the Thursday following the kiss—when she'd set up a four-o'clock appointment to talk to the Eastcreek Garden Club about sponsoring the landscaping. Nora knew these people. They were part of Harrison Archer's social set.

He knew she could talk the club into writing a nice, fat check.

He checked his watch. If she showed up at all.

She was five minutes early, but he'd already been pacing the admin office for twenty minutes, wondering if he should call her to confirm. He watched through the window as she stepped out of her car. The sun glinted on her auburn curls, picking out copper-and-gold strands that danced in the wind.

And he knew, in one piercing stab of lust, that he had been completely fooling himself.

Post-kiss wasn't going to be easier. It was going to be hell.

Growling softly at the painful tightness in his jeans, he turned away from the window and poured himself a cup of coffee.

Maybe he'd gone too long without a woman. It had been almost three and a half years. He'd assumed that because he had no interest in emotional intimacy, no desire for even the least hint of commitment, he hadn't healed. Wasn't ready.

Well, his heart might still be lying around his chest in numb, useless pieces. But apparently his body was fixed and good to go.

The door opened, letting a new shaft of sunlight in. He looked up, realizing Nora had brought Sean with her. This wasn't Sean's regular day. Had she decided she needed a buffer?

"Hi, Logan," she said, an easy lilt in her voice. She was gorgeous in a golden-brown sundress and sandals. She looked and sounded completely comfortable.

He wondered if it was artificial. Had she practiced that bland expression, that chummy tone, in front of the mirror?

Or was he really the only one who couldn't stop thinking about that night?

"Hi," he said. He smiled at Sean. "Hey, there. Back already? You just can't get enough hard labor?"

Now that Logan really looked, he saw that Sean certainly didn't mirror his mother's easy cheer. Quite the opposite. The boy looked stormy, his eyes too bright and his muscles too tight.

So Nora's nonchalance was an act. No way she could be this relaxed after driving here with this thunderhead. Logan would be willing to bet, judging from Sean's face, that he and his mom had fought bitterly all the way here, and he'd lost.

God, the kid's moods were unpredictable. Earlier this week, when he'd come for his regular shifts, he'd been in great spirits. Cooperative, easy to handle. The ideal volunteer.

Logan had thought maybe showing up at the concert had bought a little goodwill.

Ha.

"No," Sean said. "I've had plenty of work, believe me. My mom doesn't trust me alone with Milly." He glared at Nora. "She left Harry with her, though. Which doesn't make any sense, because Harry's only five."

Nora put her hand on her son's shoulder. "Sean, we're finished talking about this." She looked at Logan. "Are there any chores he can do while we have the meeting?"

Sure there were chores. There were always chores, especially now that the open house was a week from Saturday, only nine days away.

"Yeah, I think we—"

"I'm not working for free," Sean interrupted darkly. "If I do a bunch of stupid work, I'm taking it off what I owe him."

Nora's cheeks burned a bright pink. Logan saw that she was very, very angry with her son.

"All right," she said, her voice still calm. "But let's see. As long as we're counting every minute, how much do you think you owe Logan for coming to your concert last week?"

Sean's chin went up. "Nothing. You already told me he only came because he wants to have a good relationship with the school, for his programs."

She shot a look at Logan, and he knew what she was telling him. This was how she'd carried out his wishes. This was how she'd kept Sean from reading too much into Logan's appearance at the elementary school.

"Well, it was actually both," Logan said, trying to cover over the crack as smoothly as possible. "But of course you'll get credit for any work you do today. That's only fair."

Sean was unappeased. "I'd rather just sit here while you have your meeting. I have homework."

"No," Nora insisted, and her tone was firm. She obviously didn't think her bad-tempered son would be an asset in a fund-raising session. And Logan had to admit he agreed. "It's a meeting for grown-ups only. If Vic has work for you, that's where you need to be."

Logan had already texted Vic, and the manager appeared at the door promptly. "Sean's going to help with the paperwork for a little while today," Logan said.

Vic nodded without enthusiasm. He had worked with Sean often enough to recognize that scowl.

As Vic held the door open, Sean shuffled out, his annoyance evident in every bone of his skinny, hunched-over frame.

"Sorry," Nora said when they were gone. She was still going for the light tone but missing slightly. "He has good days and bad days. Obviously this is a bad day."

"Don't worry about it," Logan said.

She stood by the window, looking out. He held on to the desk, anchoring himself there so that he wouldn't walk up behind her and put his arms around her defeated shoulders.

"Nora," he began.

"Wait... Yes. They're here."

When she turned, he saw that she'd squared her shoulders again, and put her game face back on. She no longer looked like an angry, worried mom, and she certainly didn't look like a sweaty, enthusiastic volunteer.

Instead, she looked sublimely poised and gracious. She looked like what she was, big-shot Harrison Archer's elegant society widow.

She looked like a woman who would easily coax ten thousand dollars out of the East-creek Garden Club today, the Junior League tomorrow.

A fortune to Two Wings. Money the sanctuary desperately needed.

And yet, fool that he was, Logan would have locked the door and told them all to go to hell, if it meant he could, just one more time, steal a taste of those wildflower lips.

* * *

Forty-five minutes into the Garden Club meeting, Binky Fryer, the president, gave Misty Alicoate, the treasurer, the secret blink that meant *write the check.*

Nora breathed a quiet sigh of relief. She hadn't really doubted they'd donate, partly because these women sincerely loved nature— and partly because Logan Cathcart was so attractive he could charm honey from the bees with one smile.

But Nora had felt so off today, so distracted by Sean, and by seeing Logan again, that she'd been afraid she might blow it.

She met Logan's gaze over the heads of the women who were bent over their checkbook. He looked pleased. This money would pay for landscaping the acres that were open to the public, leaving him free to use the existing funds to upgrade the clinic, his dream project.

Actually, Nora would have loved to open up the Archer bank account and let it pour all over Two Wings, until every one of Logan's dream projects came true.

But a couple of things stood in her way. One was Evelyn, of course, who carefully watched Nora's every move. Whenever Nora gave away any of what Evelyn called "Harrison's money" or "the boys' inheritance," whether it was to the elementary school or to the homeless shelters, or even to the bell-ringers at Christmas, Evelyn gave her a lecture in Economics 101.

She clearly believed that Nora, unchecked, would donate them all into penury.

The other obstacle was Logan himself, who clearly was uncomfortable with the idea. He had to take money from somewhere, of course. She got the impression he'd invested heavily with his own funds, which, since he was only about twenty-eight, could hardly be limitless.

Start-up nonprofits like Two Wings couldn't possibly be self-sustaining. Bird sanctuaries would always be in need.

But he obviously didn't want to take his donations from her.

So she was delighted that she could at least help him find others willing to participate.

They were standing in front of the ticket booth, waving goodbye to the Garden Club board members sailing smoothly away in their luxury cars, when Logan's cell phone went off.

He answered it, listened for a second, then turned to Nora, his face somber.

"It's Sean," he said. "We need to get back to the sanctuary."

He started to move toward the boardwalk,

but she grabbed his wrist. "Wait. What is it? Is he okay?"

"He's fine," he said, pulling her along. "But we need to get back there. He's locked himself in the clinic."

Oh, God. Nora followed Logan as he jogged along the twisting path. She wished she'd worn her sneakers instead of these heels, which slowed her down. Why the clinic? She tried to remember what kinds of instruments the vets kept in there. What kinds of medicines?

Which birds were housed in there right now? *Oh, Sean,* she moaned silently as her heart began to pound. *Please don't do anything stupid.*

She was breathing heavily by the time they reached the clinic, though that probably was nerves, not exertion. She came to a halt awkwardly as she saw the crowd gathered around the small wooden building. Two or three volunteers watched curiously as a red-faced Vic Downing pounded on the door.

"I mean business, Sean. Open that goddamned door."

Logan touched his manager's back. "Hey," he said calmly. "Let me have a try."

Vic seemed to find it difficult to back away. Obviously things had reached a pitch here. But

Logan patted his back lightly, and that seemed to recall him to his senses.

He shook his head, then stepped down.

Logan glanced around at the others. "Okay, guys, time to get back to work. We're opening in nine days, remember? Todd, you've finished that flying cage already? Renee, what about the concrete for the path to the amphitheater?"

He didn't raise his voice, but the effect was dramatic. The teens began to move, as if they'd just woken from a sleep. Even Vic seemed to remember he was supposed to be in charge.

In about thirty seconds, only Logan and Nora remained.

"What happened?" Nora kept her voice low. She looked through the window, but the cages blocked her view. "Are we even sure he's in there?"

"Vic's seen him, apparently. Sean's put something in front of the door, so that even our master key won't get the door open. And he moved the cages, Vic says, to keep anyone from breaking the window and getting in that way."

She put her hand on her forehead. "But why? Did Vic say what happened?"

"I gather Sean was in here checking on the baby owl. Vic told him he had to get out and get back to work. He assumed Sean had done so, but the next time he tried to get into the clinic, it was locked."

She leaned against the side of the building. "Is it Hank? He loves that owl," she said. "I know that's no excuse, but..."

"No," Logan agreed grimly. "It certainly isn't."

"What can we do?"

Logan frowned. "We can take the door off the hinges, if we have to. But I'm hoping he'll open it."

She hoped so, too, but she realized that she had no idea whether he would. Her heart sped up again, as she realized she hardly knew her little boy anymore.

"Sean, it's Logan." He rapped softly on the door with his knuckles, a world of difference from Vic's aggressive pounding. "I need you to talk to me, so that I know you're okay."

Silence. Nora opened her mouth to add her voice, but Logan put up a finger. "You're too emotional," he said quietly. "You're too involved."

She nodded. It was true. She had no idea what to say, anger and anxiety creating a roiling mixture of emotions just under the surface calm.

"Sean," Logan said again, still measured. "I need to know you're okay."

"Of course I'm okay." The voice from inside was hostile, but hearty.

Nora shut her eyes in relief.

"Good," Logan said. "I'm glad to hear it."

"Why wouldn't I be okay? What do you think, I'm going to slit my wrists with the feeding tweezers?"

Logan chuckled. Nora watched him in awe. How was he able to do that? She was still trying to breathe past her heart, which seemed to have lodged about halfway up her throat.

"No," Logan admitted. "But then I also didn't think you were going to lock me out of my own clinic. So you can see why I'm not sure."

Another silence. Nora pressed her ear to the door, hoping to hear what her son was doing.

"Yeah, well." Sean sounded a little unsure of his ground. "Well, I didn't think you were going to be such an asshole about everything and treat me like such a baby. So I guess we're even."

Nora inhaled. She'd never heard her son say that word before. But Logan was grinning wryly. He looked at her briefly, shaking his head as if to say, don't have a hissy fit. It's just a word.

He turned back to the door. "Sean, you know you're going to have to open that door. I let you work here in the first place because you showed some guts the night you came over to get your bird. You didn't act like a baby that night, and you didn't get treated like one."

"So?"

"So I'm saying, if you want to be treated like a man, you're going to have to start acting like one. Open the door. Men don't hide behind a bunch of sick baby birds."

Another silence. And then the sound of a chair scraping across the floor. Nora looked at the window, and saw her son's face appear above the cages. He looked like a stranger.

The face disappeared as quickly as it came.

And then she heard the sound of a dead-bolt lock being twisted.

The door opened, and Sean came slowly out. He looked at Nora, but he didn't run up to her. He just stood on the bottom step, looking angry and proud.

Logan went up the stairs, ducked in and did a brief scan of the room. He came back out almost immediately, apparently assured that all was well.

"I didn't do a damn thing to your precious birds," Sean said. "All I wanted was to make sure Hank was all right. I wanted to talk to him for a few minutes, but Mr. Downing wouldn't let me."

"That doesn't make any difference," Logan said soberly. "Mr. Downing is your boss when you're here. You've disobeyed him, and you've crossed the line. If you can't take orders, you can't work here."

Nora could see Sean stiffen, and her heart cried out. It was too harsh a punishment. He hadn't actually hurt anything.

But then she looked at Logan, and she realized that this was what he'd meant. She was too emotional. She was too anxious for her son. She was too tangled up to make decisions that would be good for him.

"I can't work here anymore?" Sean's scowl was deep over red-rimmed eyes.

Logan shook his head. "I'm afraid not."

"Good," he said harshly. "I don't care. You think I don't know why you let me work here in the first place? You just used me to get to my mom. You want to be my mom's boyfriend."

"Sean!" Nora grabbed his shoulders. "What on earth are you talking about?"

"I'm talking about him. He's so stupid, isn't

he, Mom? As if you would ever like a guy like him."

He wheeled around and faced Logan. His hands were fists. His face was twisted and furious.

"She would never like you. Never. You know why? Because my mom loves my dad. She has never loved anybody but my dad, and she never will."

Chapter Ten

"Logan, are you busy?"

The question, posed by an earnest-faced Todd Givens, Two Wings's most experienced teen volunteer, was so ridiculous Logan had to smile.

With the open house coming a week from today, everyone at Two Wings was run ragged. The sound of hammering rang from dawn to dusk. In the offices, you waded ankle-deep in paperwork. In the clinic, you fed the birds nonstop, in an assembly line.

Logan measured out his day in five-minute increments. Five minutes to accept delivery of merchandise for the gift shop, all of which would have to be inventoried, stickered and displayed later. Five minutes to check the volunteer schedule, return phone calls, file vendor orders, arrange publicity, repair fuses, replace hoses, plant bushes, plug leaks.

Now he was heading across the east field— five minutes to meet the city inspector at the amphitheater.

And of course, somewhere in all this, they still had the birds. More birds than ever. For some perverse reason, every raptor in this part of Texas seemed to have suddenly turned kamikaze, diving into power lines and sailing into glass-sided buildings.

And they all ended up here. The only person working harder than Logan was Denver Lynch, the vet.

So yeah. Logan was busy.

"Walk with me to the amphitheater, and I can give you five minutes," he told Todd. "But talk fast."

"Okay." The boy seemed unusually somber. He was a smart, responsible kid, but he was also a jokester who kept everyone laughing while they worked. Seeing his face so solemn was strange.

Logan had thought things might settle down a little, now that Sean was gone. The teens had grumbled constantly about what a nuisance the boy was. But oddly, in the two days since Sean's departure, the mood among the volunteers had been gloomy.

Logan could relate. However perverse it might be, he, too, missed the obnoxious brat. It had been magic, the few times they'd been able to turn Sean's scowl to a smile, the few moments when his intensity had been channeled into something productive. He was moody, but he was also passionate, curious, hungry to learn.

Ten times in the past two days, Logan had picked up the phone to call Nora and see if Sean was all right. Ten times he'd resisted the urge.

Only one word accurately described the attitude he'd started to take toward Sean.

And it was a word he didn't use.

Paternal.

"So what's up, Todd?"

"Well, two things," Todd started awkwardly. "First, I wanted to give you Sean's backpack."

Logan glanced down at the small navy blue lump Todd held toward him. "His backpack?"

"Yeah. He left it in the break room. I figured you could get it back to him."

Logan took it and slung it over his shoulder. "And the second thing?"

"Um." Todd's pace slowed down. "Well, it's about Sean, too."

Logan checked the time. He still had four minutes, and they were at the peak of the little hill. He could see the amphitheater, nestled in the small basin of land below them, and the inspector hadn't yet arrived.

He stopped walking. Todd stopped, too, and shoved his hands in his pockets.

"Okay," Logan said. "What is it?"

"It's…well, it's kind of awkward…." He stopped again.

This attitude was darn odd, and gave Logan an uncomfortable premonition of trouble. Todd was witty and confident, well aware of his natural talents.

Timid was not Todd Givens's natural state.

Logan tapped his watch. "Tick, tock," he said.

"I know. It's just that… I've been thinking about what Sean said, you know, the day he got so mad and locked himself in the clinic." Todd's rugged cheekbones flushed slightly. "You know. About you and…you and his dad."

Logan nodded slowly. No wonder Todd was blushing. It wasn't what Sean had said about

Logan and Harrison that had made its way like wildfire through the grapevine.

It was what Sean had said about Logan and Nora.

Logan nodded. "What about it?"

Todd focused on the ground, kicking his heel into the grass. "It's just that…" He finally looked at Logan. "I think I know why he said that. I think it was because of me."

Logan raised his eyebrows. "You?"

"Yeah. I think he heard me talking to Matt. I mean, we were joking around, you know, being stupid. Matt was bitch—complaining about Sean, about how the kid was so stuck on himself. And I said…"

He paused and gazed into the middle distance awkwardly, still nudging the grass with his heel. "Remember, I didn't know he could hear me. But I said there was no way you would have let Sean work here in the first place if his mom hadn't been so hot. I kind of said that you wanted to…you know…get with her."

Get with her?

With effort, Logan kept his groan on the inside, but…

Damn it.

He knew what teenage boys were like then they were alone. Their language was foul, and their conversations focused exclusively on sex. *Get with her?* Logan would lay money that wasn't the expression Todd had used.

"Are you sure Sean heard you?"

Todd nodded, clearly in abject misery now, as if he'd finally reached the hard part.

Good grief. Could this story possibly get any worse?

"How do you know he heard you?"

"I guess he'd been on the other side of the owl enclosure. You know how he is about those owls. He came out of nowhere, and he came out swinging."

"He hit you?"

"Well, he tried. Matt held him off with one hand. He's just a puny little kid, you know, so it wasn't a big deal. But then Matt said something like, why didn't Sean just go away. Why didn't he go get his dad's gun and shoot something."

Logan's insides ran cold. "Ah, hell. *Todd.*"

"I know." Todd dug his hand through his hair. "I'm sorry, Logan. Matt didn't want me to tell you. He said you'd be pissed. But I don't know. It didn't seem right, Sean getting all the grief, when we were at least partly responsible."

When Nora looked at the calendar, she couldn't quite believe it had been merely two days since Sean had been banished from the sanctuary.

It felt like forever.

She didn't blame Logan for his decision. She knew it was the only choice he could make, really. His permits for handling and rehabbing the birds depended on his maintaining a professional, safe environment. He had to protect the wildlife, and his other workers, too.

Plus, Sean needed to learn that actions had consequences. If people continued to excuse his behavior because they felt sorry for him, he'd start believing he could get away with...

Her fingers trembled, and she put down the calendar she'd been holding. She'd been about to say he'd think he could get away with murder.

Just as his father had.

She leaned back against the spindles of the Boston rocker and shut her eyes, trying to calm her pulse. Ordinarily her delft-blue reading room was her favorite spot in the hacienda. From its window she could see the whole bricked courtyard, and enjoy its transformation from season to season.

Right now, the courtyard was glorious with spring. The bougainvillea that had been trained over the arches was rich with purple blooms, and the pink hibiscus along the wall had flowers as big as dinner plates.

The comfy little reading nook had originally been intended as a dressing room carved out between his-her boudoirs of the patron and his wife. But Nora had claimed the space immediately after her marriage and moved the master bedroom down the hall. As the boys arrived, she'd arranged their bedrooms on either side of her bookshelf-lined haven.

It was perfect. While Harrison was alive, she'd been able to sit quietly and read every night, insulated from the rancher "boys" who came to visit Harrison and feast on Milly's food.

Nora had nothing in common with those well-fed, self-important, middle-aged millionaires. They could talk all night about cattle and politics, and the politics of cattle.

She always made her obligatory appearance at dinner, where she did her best to impersonate an adoring trophy wife, although she knew she looked more like a stray kitten Harrison had picked up in an alley somewhere.

Still, she was twenty-five years younger than her husband, and that apparently was trophy enough. The men complimented her, held out her chair and called her "sweetheart," then winked an indulgent goodbye when she excused herself to "check on the boys."

She loved the proximity to Sean and Harry. They were so used to her quiet presence that they often forgot she was here, and she overheard a million adorable, foolish conversations that went straight into the lockbox of her heart.

Tonight, Sean was supposed to be practicing the guitar, but his plunking sounded like a halfhearted dirge. Harry had come in to listen, and of course pretty soon they were doing a lot more talking than practicing.

She'd almost drifted off when she heard Harry mention Two Wings.

"I think Mr. Logan would let you come back, Sean. If you went over there and told him you were sorry."

Sean made a disgusted sound. "No way."

"Why not?" Harry must have reached out to touch the guitar, because it let out a sudden cascade of notes in the key of horrible.

"Don't touch that, dork." The guitar fell silent, and then Nora heard the sound of Harry tapping something, beating out an intricate rhythm. She was going to have to get him a set of drums, she could tell.

"You're going to break my picks," Sean said querulously. And then the tapping stopped.

But Harry didn't seem chastened. He started humming, and then the springs of the bed began to squeak. Nora smiled to herself, picturing the little boy standing on the bed, bopping unabashedly to his own music.

Harry's good humor was like an endless crystal spring, hidden deep inside him. She wished he could share some of it with Sean right now. She'd even be glad to borrow a little herself.

"So," Harry said raggedly, one word for each bounce, "why not?"

"Because. You should have seen how mad Logan was. I'm lucky he didn't call the cops."

"The cops?" The squeaking continued, and Harry's words still came out jerky. "That would have been exciting. Don't you think?"

"No." Sean's surly syllable was muffled, as if he had his face in the pillow.

"But you would have been like…like a desperado."

"I wasn't a desperado, genius. It wasn't like that. It wasn't cool at all. It was scary. Everyone was really, really mad."

Harry's bouncing stopped. When he spoke, his voice was humble. "You were scared, Sean?"

"Yeah, I was scared. It was like…you know

when you do something without really thinking, and then you realize there's no way out? You're stuck?"

Harry was silent a minute. "You mean like when you stand in line to ride the roller coaster? And then you don't really want to go, but there are people behind you?"

Nora expected Sean to laugh at the little boy's struggle to put the deed into a five-year-old's context. But to her surprise, Sean didn't so much as snigger.

"Yeah," Sean said. "Yeah, kind of like that. Only worse, because people aren't just thinking you're a baby. They're thinking you're a bad person."

"You're not a bad person!" Harry sounded highly indignant.

"I know. But I did a bad thing. A really bad thing."

"Yeah, but remember? Mom said Daddy did a bad thing, but that didn't make him a bad man. Remember?"

Nora's fingers tightened on the arms of the rocker.

"Yeah, I remember," Sean said dismissively. "But that's because she loves him. Most people think Daddy was super bad. Don't people say stuff to you about him?"

"Stuff like what?"

"Bad stuff. Mean stuff."

"No." Harry sounded bewildered. "My friends are nice."

"Well, mine aren't."

Nora closed her eyes. Harrison would be devastated to know he'd brought his little boy so much pain.

As she was.

But what was done was done. Fate had dealt them a rotten hand. It did that to lots of people. The challenge was to survive. The challenge was to piece together a happy life anyhow.

The boys were very quiet for a while. She thought about going in and seeing if they'd talk to her, but Sean had just revealed more to his little brother in two minutes than he'd said to her in the past two days.

She'd tried to work through it with him, right after they'd gotten home from Two Wings. She'd very carefully explained that he had nothing to worry about. She had loved their father, and she loved Sean and Harry. She always would. Nothing, ever, would change that. They would always be the most important people in the world to her.

And she'd also assured him Logan had definitely not had any ulterior motives for letting Sean work at Two Wings. Logan needed help, and Sean owed him for damages. Logan had been impressed with the way Sean handled himself the night he came to retrieve his bird.

It was as simple as that.

She wasn't going to add a punishment, she said. She knew that being banished from Two Wings was punishment enough. His dark, pain-filled eyes had confirmed the truth of that, but he'd spoken hardly a word.

The next day, she'd taken him to the therapist, and when the hour was up the doctor had assured her Sean was remorseful about what he'd done, and he seemed to understand that it was wrong. To the therapist, those seemed to be the cogent points.

But Nora still hoped Sean would find a way to talk it out. So she waited, hoping Harry's open heart, and the trust between the brothers, would make her elder son feel safe enough to share his feelings.

Harry wasn't a fan of silence. After a couple of minutes, he began to hum again.

And then, out of nowhere, he cried out triumphantly, "I got it! Dickey Barnes!"

"Dickey Barnes," Sean mumbled sleepily, "is a dork."

"No, he's not," Harry said, ever loyal to his kindergarten pals. "But anyhow, Dickey has an older brother."

"Who is also a dork."

"Yeah. Gil's mean. He's always in trouble. Dickey's dad wasn't going to let Gil drive the car anymore, but he signed a contract, so now he can."

"What kind of contract?" Sean's voice sounded slightly more awake.

"You know. A list of the stuff he'll do. I promise to take out the garbage every day. I promise not to say s-h-i-t in front of my mom. I promise not to call Dickey a turd. Stuff like that."

For flourish, Harry strummed the guitar again, apparently forgetting he wasn't allowed. When Sean didn't protest, Nora knew he must be deep in thought.

Her throat tightened. Should she stop this right now? She knew how unlikely it was that Logan would ever change his mind about Sean.

Gil Barnes had been granted a driving reprieve, not because of the contract, but because his parents adored him. Parents tried to find an answer. Parents seized on any chance to forgive and say yes, and make their children smile again.

But Logan wasn't Sean's dad.

And he'd made it clear he didn't want to be.

So writing a contract wouldn't open the doors of Two Wings, which was of course what Sean was hoping. He desperately wanted to see the birds again. The owlet Hank, especially.

But maybe she should let him write the contract anyhow. It would be good for him. He'd have to think it through. He'd have to articulate exactly what he'd done wrong. He'd have to analyze his behavior, his attitude, his tones, and identify which specific ones had gotten him into trouble.

And then he'd have to build a detailed picture of the boy he wanted to be.

"Yeah, we should definitely make a contract for you," Harry said happily, well aware that this would buy him more precious time in his big brother's hallowed presence. "Promise Mr. Logan that you'll do everything right, and you won't do anything wrong."

Nora heard Sean's desk drawer slide open, and the clatter of someone rummaging for a pen.

"Okay," Sean said. "I guess I'll try it. How long is Gil's contract, do you know?"

"Long," Harry said dramatically. "Maybe three pages. But he didn't do anything crazy, like kidnap birds. So yours should probably be like...ten."

Chapter Eleven

As soon as he realized he was dying, Harrison had set Bull's Eye up to practically run itself. He knew Nora had no interest in, or talent for, the ranching business. She'd never pretended otherwise. She found the cattle end of it sad, and the quarter horses intimidating.

It was one of the failings that disgusted Evelyn most, because, if Harrison had left the ranch to his sister, she would have delighted in every trivial detail of the daily decisions.

Even so, Nora still had to get together with bankers, lawyers, foremen and accountants occasionally. She hoped that, if word got out she was having lunch with Jim Stilling, the Archer family attorney, Evelyn would assume it was just one of those boring meetings.

In reality, this early Monday lunch was Nora's first legal consultation to prepare for any possible custody battle to come.

Jim didn't specialize in custody issues, but he was one of the few lawyers in Eastcreek she thought she could trust.

It might sound paranoid, but the Archer/Gellner names carried a lot of weight around here. And not just because lineage and acreage were worshiped in Texas. Half the lawyers and judges and police officers in Eastcreek had gone to college on scholarships from the Archer Foundation or the Gellner Family Charitable Trust.

Not many of them would risk standing across a courtroom from a hostile Evelyn Archer Gellner.

The lunch on the sunny, flowered patio of Aunt Violet's Veranda—one of Nora's favorite local restaurants—had gone well. Jim was smart and low-key, and entirely on her side. His father had been Harrison's lawyer for decades, and Jim had taken over shortly after Paul died. So he'd been on scene when Harrison married Nora. He'd written the prenup she'd been happy to sign.

A prenup that Harrison had emphatically ignored in his will.

Jim Stilling understood, better than most, how completely Harrison had trusted Nora. He knew what Harrison's wishes had been about the boys, too.

"I don't think you'll have any real trouble," he said as they stood to leave. "But I'll ask around for some names just in case. Maybe someone in Austin."

She smiled. "Yes, someone who hasn't ever heard of Eastcreek, if possible. I like to be sure where their allegiance lies." She tucked her hand under his elbow as they moved through the tables and hanging baskets of plants. "She won't do it, will she, Jim?"

"She would be foolish if she did," Jim said. "She'd have to demonstrate that you were unfit. And I can't imagine anything harder to prove than that."

"Even if Sean—"

"Even if Sean is being a jackass," he said firmly.

Over lunch, she had told him all about Sean's moods, as well as his problems at Two Wings. Evelyn would hear about Sean's commandeering the clinic, sooner or later, and Nora knew what spin Sean's angry aunt would put on it.

"You haven't neglected him, or put him in danger." Jim squeezed her hand briefly, a show of support she appreciated. "That's what matters."

"Yes, but Evelyn absolutely hates the idea that he's been working at Two Wings. Her attitude toward Logan Cathcart is—"

"Is downright nasty." Jim nodded. "Yeah, I've heard all about it, unfortunately."

Even Jim had heard? Nora dodged a rabbit-ear fern that had been hung too low. Of course even Jim, she answered herself. The Stillings were as Old Texas as the Archers. "What did you hear?"

"She thinks you're having a torrid affair with Cathcart," Jim said blandly. He held open the swinging white wrought-iron gate to let her pass through. "Are you?"

She laughed, caught totally by surprise. "Well, that's blunt," she said.

He shrugged. "Lawyers ask questions. It's the best way to get information, actually. Infinitely preferable to secondhand gossip."

"No," she said. "I'm not. Why? Would it give Evelyn ammunition against me if I were?"

"Nope. Not unless you were going at it right in front of the boys, or while you were cracked out on drugs. Even widows are allowed to have sex, Nora, here in the twenty-first century."

"I know," she said. But she was aware that she didn't sound convinced. Because she wasn't. She could easily see how a judge might be persuaded that a lover was distracting, stealing Nora's attention, making her careless with the kids.

Or that her divided affections would be disturbing two children who were already desperately insecure.

"The reason I asked, actually," Jim said in a low voice, "is that we're about to—" He broke off, and held out his hand. "Cathcart! Nice to see you."

As the two men shook hands, Nora flushed and tried to smile normally. How could she have missed Logan, standing there by his truck?

"Hi, Nora," he said, holding out his hand to her. "I'm glad to run into you. I need to return Sean's backpack."

She accepted his hand, though she had a feeling her palms were damp.

"Hi," she said awkwardly.

"Sorry, guys, but do you mind if I take off?" Jim put his hand on her shoulder. "I've got a hearing in half an hour, and you know what a stickler Judge Corrigan is."

She couldn't tell if Jim was making the whole hearing thing up. He certainly hadn't mentioned it before. But she couldn't very well protest. They'd met up at the restaurant, so they each had their own cars.

"Sure, that's fine." She kissed his cheek. "Thanks for the advice."

After a few more polite words, she and Logan were alone. While she searched for something appropriate to say, he opened the passenger door, pulled Sean's navy backpack out and handed it to her.

"Apparently Sean left this in the break room," he said. "I thought about bringing it by the ranch, but—"

"Oh, well, that's okay. No problem. He has another one, and he didn't even mention this one was missing." She hugged the backpack to her chest nervously. She was talking too much, saying nothing. "But thanks. I appreciate it."

He shut the car door. Then he leaned against the hood, and shoved his hands in his pockets. He looked edgy, as if he needed to say something he didn't want to say.

She thought she knew what it was, and she tried to spare him the discomfort. "Logan, I

want to apologize again for Sean. The clinic—
and the things he said. I don't know what got
into him. He's—"

"I do."

She broke off, frowning. "You do what?"

"I know what got into him. Todd Givens
brought the backpack to me yesterday, but that
was just an excuse to talk privately. He wanted
to confess that he and his buddy Matt were the
ones who got Sean so stirred up."

"Todd?" She could hardly believe it. He
seemed like a nice kid, and he was terrific
with the birds. Sean had a mild case of hero-
worship for the older boy, and wanted desperately to learn his secrets.

"How? What on earth could they have
done?"

"I gather they are the ones who put the idea
in Sean's head about...about us. They made
some comments, and apparently Sean overheard them."

"Oh, God."

"I know." Logan gave her a half smile.
"Makes more sense now, right? No boy is
going to sit idly by while people talk trash
about his mom."

She shook her head. "Not in Texas, anyhow."

"Not anywhere. I don't think I would have

blamed Sean one bit if he'd beaten the tar out of Todd. Unfortunately, he's not big enough to do that, so…"

She took a moment to digest the news. She was embarrassed, of course. She wondered what the teenagers had seen—what vibes they'd sensed—that made them say such things. Was she that transparent? Could everyone tell she was a lonely, frustrated widow hankering after the cute guy next door?

The sad truth was, she'd been lonely and frustrated for years before she'd become a widow. Had everyone been able to see that, too?

"But still," she said, trying to view the situation objectively, "what Sean did was wrong. Even if he was upset, locking himself in the clinic was just plain dangerous."

"True." Logan nodded ruefully. He took a breath, as if to say something, then hesitated.

"It's okay," she said. "I know you can't let him come back. I really do understand."

"No, I can't," he agreed ruefully. "I can't risk letting him work with the birds. I was flirting with danger anyhow, because we don't ever take volunteers younger than eighteen."

"I know."

Her heart ached for Sean, but, if she were

completely honest, she'd have to admit some of the pain was her own. She had loved working at Two Wings. Over the past few days, she'd still been providing design help and creating lesson plans, but it was done by e-mail now. She sent files to Vic Downing, who forwarded them to Logan for approval, then sent them back to her.

All neatly sanitized, impersonal. A contribution, but one stripped of all the teeming, chaotic life of the sanctuary itself.

Of course, there was no point in trying to kid anyone. Mostly she missed Logan. But she also missed the urgency, the rush to bring everything together in time for the grand opening. She missed being outside, getting dirty. The birds crying, the wind in the trees.

She missed the sense of purpose. The struggle to preserve life, even when it was a struggle lost, felt real in a way nothing in her life ever had.

Except the boys.

Which was why she had to do right by them, at any cost. Theirs were the lives that had been entrusted to her. She had to protect them from whatever threatened their happiness.

Even if the threat came from her own heart.

Logan chewed a minute on the inside of his

lip. Then he took a breath. "Do you think he'd be willing to work in the gift shop?"

She wasn't sure how to respond. Could he really be serious?

"Of course he would. Would you be willing to have him?"

"Maybe. But think about it. It might actually be even more difficult, being so close, but not being allowed to work with the birds."

"Yes, that would be hard."

Almost as hard, she thought, as it would be for her to work next to Logan and know that he would never kiss her again. But she'd endure that a million times over, rather than never see him at all.

"He wants so desperately to be forgiven, Logan. For that, he'd do anything." She smiled. "In fact, Sean and Harry have created a contract, listing all the things he'll do differently, if only you'll let him come back. There's a list of words he won't say. Tones he won't take. And he says he'll do anything. Sell tickets, or answer the phone, or clean the sinks."

"Clean the sinks?"

"Yeah." She wished she had a copy of the foolish document with her. She could never capture its poignant sincerity in her description. "Harry insisted that offering to clean the toilets sounded more humble, but Sean decided to write down *sinks* instead. That way, he said, he could raise his offer to include the toilets later, if he needed to."

Logan laughed. "A tough little negotiator. Sounds like Harrison trying to talk me into selling the land. He sure is a chip off the old block, isn't he?"

She sobered instantly.

"In some ways, he is," she acknowledged. "But that's not a bad thing, Logan. Harrison was a loyal, loving man."

Logan nodded slowly. "I know."

He gave her a searching look that made the butterflies begin to beat their wings. His gaze swept over her face, down her body and back again to her eyes.

"But let's be honest with each other, Nora. If I let Sean come back, it won't be because of his dad. It will be because he's also very much his mother's son."

That Friday, on the final afternoon before the open house, Logan stopped in at the gift shop on his way to the sanctuary. Rachel had asked him to grab Nora, who had been there since about three, helping Sean.

Logan stretched his shoulders, wishing he

had time to swallow an aspirin. He couldn't believe it was only six o'clock. It felt like midnight. He'd spent hours in the sun, first decorating the amphitheater, then training the newly graduated docents.

He'd spent half the afternoon grilling them to be sure they knew the correct answers to the questions visitors were likely to ask. During the open house, one docent would be stationed at each different raptor enclosure, and needed to be an expert on that bird.

Some of them were; some definitely weren't.

But he couldn't shovel any more knowledge into their tired brains now. He'd finally set them free, much to everyone's relief.

He let himself in through the storage area at the back of the shop. "Nora?"

There was no answer. He wondered if she'd left early. Had there been an emergency at home? But she wouldn't have left without telling him. She knew how much he needed every single man-hour.

In fact, he wasn't sure how he would have managed if he hadn't relented about Sean. Since he'd come back Monday afternoon, chastened and pink-cheeked, the kid had been true to every word of his crazy contract. He'd worked like a soldier, getting the gift shop ready almost single-handedly. He'd obeyed every edict, and he'd never said a disrespectful word.

Logan moved through the boxes and cartons into the store proper. It looked great, with stuffed toys piled in every nook, puppets dangling from the ceiling, and a whole reading corner for the little ones, complete with chairs shaped like flamingos.

"Nora? You here?"

But the only person in the shop was Sean. The boy was perched on the window seat, carefully affixing price stickers to a five-hundred-count carton of tiny plastic frogs, ladybugs and lizards. Though it was clearly a mind-numbing task, he seemed content.

He wore his iPod's earphones and sang softly along to his music. Occasionally his bony shoulders twitched, as if he'd like to get up and dance.

Watching the boy, Logan instinctively froze in place, as he might have done if he'd come upon a heron in the wild. He didn't want to make a move or utter a sound that would disturb the natural grace and innocence of the scene.

Without warning, Sean lifted one of the lizards high in the air, and his voice grew louder.

He sang out emphatically, grinding out the words with a macho rumble, and wiggling the lizard as if it were the leader of a rock band.

Just then, movement outside the window distracted the boy. The singing ceased, as if someone had flipped a switch. He dropped the lizard into the "done" box and climbed onto his knees to see what was going on.

Logan looked, too. Denver Lynch was arriving, returning one of the peregrine falcons who had just recovered from surgery. Nora, who must have been waiting outside the gift shop door, hurried over to help. Todd loped out, too, coming across the boardwalk from the sanctuary. Together they began unloading the falcon's crate.

Sean leaned forward, his hands gripping the marble sill so hard his knuckles turned white. He watched every move, transfixed. The yearning was so intense Logan could almost feel it in his own chest. He wondered if Sean might sneak out, just this once, just to catch a glimpse of the falcon.

But he didn't. As Denver, Todd and Nora began to move beyond his vision, Sean reached up and touched his fingertips to the glass.

When they were gone, he knelt there another long minute, staring helplessly at the empty parking lot. Then, slowly, as if he had to force himself to do it, he returned to his box of toys and his endless stack of stickers.

His face was stoic. His fingers were as careful as ever, applying stickers one after the other.

But the singing had died.

Logan inhaled, shocked by the rush of feeling that swept through him. It wasn't pity, exactly. And it was more than respect, though he felt that, too.

No, when he looked at this odd little boy, with those messy red curls shining in the sunlight, and that tiger heart pounding in his scrawny chest, Logan felt something more like…tenderness.

For a minute, he couldn't breathe. He turned and left the shop.

God help him. Was he crazy? He'd done the one thing he'd sworn he'd never do.

The one thing he hadn't even thought he was capable of doing anymore.

He had let himself start to care.

Chapter Twelve

"Logan, I'm sorry we're late." As a soft hand was placed on his back, Logan turned. He was still holding the feeding puppets he'd been demonstrating for a group of Girl Scouts, the last official group tour of the open house.

The hand belonged to Susannah Maxwell, a young peach grower who had been one of the first people in Eastcreek's power structure to actually make him feel welcome.

May was an intense month in her season, so he hadn't been sure she'd be able to show up. Plus, she was about fifteen months pregnant.

He made a stab at hugging her, a gesture that had become almost impossible, then laughed.

"I'm glad you're here, but are you sure it's safe for you to be this far from an obstetrician?"

"I'm fine," she said, laying her hands comfortably across the conspicuous swell. "I told the baby he had to wait till after the open house."

"You *told* the baby?" Trent, her husband, laughed. He wrapped his arms around her from behind and nuzzled her neck.

It was the only way to get truly close to a woman nine months pregnant. Logan remembered doing it with Rebecca.

He was surprised to realize that, for the first time, the memory didn't come paired with its usual wrench of anger.

Guess he didn't have the time—or the inclination—to resent the past today. Today, the future held all the power.

"So I guess you've hatched a lot of bird babies around here, Cathcart," Trent said with a grin that proclaimed him the happiest man in Eastcreek. "Think you can handle a human baby, if it turns out Susannah doesn't control the universe after all?"

"I told you, I'm not going into labor tonight!" Susannah tilted her head to allow Trent free access to every inch of her throat. "I asked him to wait, and he's going to be a very good, patient little baby. The complete opposite of his daddy."

"And his mommy." Trent nipped at Susannah's shoulder, chuckling. "I'm not sure patience is going to be in this kid's DNA package, sweetheart."

Sean came trotting up then, holding his little brother, Harry, by the hand. "Logan, the band's ready to start playing, and Mom says she's through face painting."

Logan glanced at the western horizon, surprised to see that the sky was orange behind the black silhouettes of the trees. Nora had been painting owls and eagles on the cheeks of school kids all day, but the tours and education part of the open house officially ended at sundown.

Now the feasting, dancing and well-deserved fun could begin. As soon as Logan said the magic words.

"Thanks," he said. "Tell your mom I'll—"

And then he noticed that Sean's face had gone as red as the western sky. He frowned. "Everything okay?"

Trent, apparently, had realized Sean's problem faster than Logan did. That made sense, of course, because Trent *was* Sean's problem.

Watching the boy's shoulders stiffen, Logan

winced, remembering suddenly that Trent Maxwell was the man Sean's father had wanted to kill.

"Hi, Sean," Trent said in a tone so close to normal that Logan had to give him acting points. "Hey, Harry. How's your mom?"

"Hi, Mr. Maxwell," Harry said merrily. Harry probably didn't even remember the day Sean had found Harrison down at Green Fern Pond, crazed with grief about his dead son, oblivious to the living, breathing sons who still needed him.

"Mom's okay." Harry babbled on merrily. "She's talking to Aunt Evelyn about getting a job. Aunt Evelyn doesn't want her to." He pointed to his cheek. "She gave me a penny-green falcon."

"Peregrine falcon," Sean corrected through tight lips, obviously squeezing Harry's hand to get him to shut up.

He flicked a quick, inscrutable glance toward Trent, then turned to Logan. "We should probably get back. But Mom thinks you should come say something to everyone so they can start dancing. They have a microphone for you, up by the band."

"Okay. Tell her I'll be right there."

"It was good to see you guys," Trent said,

giving Sean a smile with some extra warmth in it. "You know, Sean, I wanted to talk to you anyhow."

Sean frowned. "Why?"

"Because we're going to need a lot of help at Everly this summer, when the peaches come in. Sue and I were wondering whether you have any time you could spare to help at one of the roadside stands."

"You want me to work at Everly?" Sean sounded incredulous.

Trent lifted one shoulder. "Well, only if you want to. Logan told us what a hard worker you are, and that's exactly the kind of help we need."

Sean clearly wanted to look at Logan, to see if it could possibly be true that he'd been given a good report. But he wouldn't let himself. He kept his head frozen, his frown in place.

"I don't know," he said. "I'll have to ask my mom."

"Sure." Trent accepted the answer with a laid-back ease. "That's cool. Just let me know."

The boys blended back into the crowd milling about on the amphitheater stage. Logan watched them until they were swallowed up by the taller adults.

"I should probably get this show on the

road," he said to Trent and Susannah, who were also watching the little boys walk away.

"I hope it was okay to say you'd spoken well of him," Trent said cautiously. "How is he working out? I talk to Nora now and then, and it sounds rough."

"There are some bad days," Logan said, as honestly as he could. "But there are also some good days. He's a solid kid, under it all. I'm hoping that'll be enough to see him through."

"And his mother adores him," Susannah added. She rubbed her belly thoughtfully. "That's got to help."

"Yes." Logan understood that Nora's unflinching love was like a raft, keeping Sean afloat whether he knew it or not. "Nora never gives up on him. She's a pretty amazing woman."

He saw Trent and Susannah exchange a knowing glance, and he laughed. "I meant she's an amazing *mother*."

"Of course you did." Trent smiled smoothly. "Come on, I want to dance with my wife, so let's get that band going."

The amphitheater was party central. The high school jazz band was set up in the pit just below the amphitheater stage, prepared with an evening's worth of wildlife songs, ev-

erything from "Bye Bye Birdie" to "The Lion
Sleeps Tonight."

The hors d'oeuvres, donated by a local ca-
terer, were laid out on long, white tables. The
dancing would take place on the stage.

The place looked terrific. Volunteers had
strung paper lanterns and white Christmas
lights everywhere, including the branches of
the nearby trees.

The turnout from the community was amazing. Logan saw just about everyone he knew—
and quite a few new faces, too—milling about
on the stage.

His eyes kept scanning until he found Nora.
She was, as the boys had reported, standing
with Evelyn and a couple of Evelyn's older
friends. It didn't seem to be a festive gathering.
Nora's smile looked fake—funny, he thought,
that he could tell that, even from twenty feet
away. And Evelyn looked downright grim.

Grimmer than usual, which was saying
something.

Her friends looked on with avid curiosity as
Evelyn held forth about something.

Nora needed to get out of there. He passed
right by the microphone and kept walking until
he got to the cluster of women.

As he approached, he heard Evelyn talking

forcefully. He couldn't hear the words, but it reinforced his intuition. Nora didn't need this harridan's scolding tonight. Tonight was a celebration.

"Hey," he said as he reached her side. He didn't wait for Evelyn to finish her sentence, which of course annoyed the hell out of the woman. Good. She stared daggers at him, and he enjoyed ignoring them.

He hadn't had a chance to speak to Nora all day. Suddenly he couldn't wait. "Can I steal you for a second, Nora? We've got an issue, and I need your help."

"Of course." She smiled politely to the women. "I'm so sorry. Please excuse me."

The women had no choice but to accept their dismissal, though Evelyn obviously resented it deeply. With her beady black eyes boring into their backs, Logan and Nora walked off together, shoulder to shoulder, their fingers brushing lightly.

When they were a few feet away, she spoke under her breath. "There's no issue, is there?"

"Of course not." He chuckled. "If you were having fun, I apologize. But frankly...you looked like a goldfish surrounded by piranhas, and I just couldn't watch you get eaten alive."

"That's pretty much how it felt," she admitted. She made a low rumble of frustration. "Evelyn was about to spoil tonight for me, and that would have been a shame. Everything has gone so well today."

They reached the edge of the stage, where his microphone lay, waiting for him to make the opening remarks. He didn't pick it up. Instead he watched Nora. The sunset tipped her curls with a golden fire, and her eyes were lit up, too.

She looked wonderful when she acted this way. He wondered if this was how she used to be, before Harrison, before Evelyn, before she gave her life away.

"Evelyn seemed even more sour than usual. What had you done to tick her off this time?"

Nora shrugged. "Basically, I didn't bow to her superior wisdom."

He raised his eyebrows. "The nerve."

"Yeah. I know. But I——" She smiled, and began again. "About an hour ago, Jolie Harper stopped by where I was face painting. She's the music teacher at the elementary school. She told me there's an opening for the director of the band camp this summer. She was going to do it, but something came up. She was hoping I might be interested."

"And are you?"

The wistful yearning in her face was answer enough, but she nodded. "I'd love it," she said. "It's what I've always wanted to do. But Evelyn was there, and unfortunately she thinks it's a terrible idea."

"Why? Because of Sean?"

"I guess so." Nora shook her head. "That's the excuse she gives, anyhow. She actually answered for me. She told Jolie that of course I wouldn't consider it."

What a bitch, he thought. But he waited. Nora was clearly angry, and he had a feeling she'd stood up for herself quite well on her own.

"And I guess that was just…too much," she went on. "I try hard to get along with Evelyn, really, I do. Maybe too hard. But this time, I wasn't in the mood. So I told Jolie I'd love to take over the camp."

He let out a laugh.

"Way to go," he said. "Felt good?"

She grinned sheepishly. "Felt terrific. I'll be paying for this insubordination for a long, long time." She wrinkled her nose like a very naughty, very adorable schoolgirl. "But I have to admit…it was worth it."

He glanced back toward where they'd left the older woman. It was an unpleasant surprise to see her still standing there, still staring at Nora with an expression that could only be called malevolent.

He suddenly wanted to wrap Nora in his arms and protect her from the rays of that gaze.

Actually, he had to admit, there was nothing sudden about it. He always wanted to wrap Nora Archer in his arms.

"Nora!" Denver Lynch came rushing up to them. "I've been looking for you. I was hoping you'd give me the first dance."

Logan had to be careful not to let his reaction show on his face. But damn it. Denver looked breathless and eager, as if dancing with Nora would be a dream come true.

Also, dressed like this in street clothes, Denver looked like a completely different person. Logan hadn't ever seen him out of his veterinarian's white coat.

In the eighteen months he'd known Denver, Logan hadn't once considered whether the vet was a good-looking man. The birds didn't care, and Logan didn't care, so it just hadn't ever registered.

Until now.

Now he saw that Denver was probably what most women considered fantastic-looking. He had green eyes and blond hair, and he was playing both up shamelessly in that green-and-gold plaid dress shirt.

Nora was smiling. She looked quickly over her shoulder, to where Evelyn still stood. The older woman's dark gaze had never wavered. Nora flushed, and Logan saw her shoulders sag.

Damn it, Nora. Dance.

He wished he'd asked her first. He wished he were as rich and slick as the irritatingly handsome vet. But as he watched her grapple with the decision, he discovered that he didn't care who she danced with, as long as she had some fun tonight.

She's just a bitter old bitch, Nora. Don't let her scare you.

For a moment Logan thought she might lose her nerve. But then she squared her shoulders and faced Denver Lynch with a smile that damn near knocked the man down.

"Thanks," she said. "I'd love to."

An hour later, that first dance with Denver Lynch was the only time Nora had said yes all night.

Whatever little gust of defiance had briefly filled her sails had died almost immediately. Evelyn's hostility was palpable. The woman seethed from her corner of the stage, pulsing there like some kind of judgmental nineteenth-century duenna. She obviously felt that Nora dishonored Harrison's memory by dancing at all.

Nora probably could have disregarded Evelyn, if her sister-in-law's antiquated ideas had been the only consideration. Evelyn had complained about Nora's decisions every day since Harrison's death. The funeral was wrong, the casket was inferior. Over the months, the clothes Nora wore were too colorful. She laughed too loudly at public events.

A full year of formal mourning, complete with sackcloth and ashes, wouldn't have appeased the woman. She *might* have been satisfied if Nora had climbed onto her dead husband's funeral pyre, as some ancient cultures had dictated a widow should do, but nothing short of total immolation would suffice.

The deeper problem tonight was that Nora didn't really feel like dancing. She was still too conflicted. In her heart, she, too, felt guilty that she lived, laughed, danced…while Harrison lay dead in the ground. She didn't have Evelyn's Victorian delusions about mourning, but six months was a very short time to have been a widow.

Harrison had been much loved and was much missed—and she wouldn't want anyone to think otherwise.

In spite of all that…she had to be honest. If Logan had asked her, she might have been tempted.

But he didn't ask.

And maybe that was just as well. Sean's outburst the other day had been precipitated by Todd Givens's gossip, but that cry had come from the heart.

She has never loved anybody but my dad, and she never will.

He wasn't ready.

He wouldn't have wanted to deny her any happiness, but children didn't think in those terms. He was watchful, suspicious, quick to judge.

He no longer had the blind trust a child should have. He had seen a beloved father turn into a dangerous stranger. He had been just old enough, the day he'd found his father with the gun, to look at the situation and decide it meant that Harrison had loved his first, dead son better than he loved the two who had come after.

He had been too young to understand how many different kinds of love can coexist in the complicated labyrinth of the human heart. He still was.

So when Denver Lynch asked her to dance a second time, she turned him down. And then she turned down Trent, and Chase, and half a dozen sweet, well-intentioned men.

She thought about leaving early. It had been a long day—a long month of preparation, too. The giddiness of earlier in the evening had worn off, and she realized that she was exhausted.

So when she saw the odd man in the trench coat and a baseball cap heading toward her, her first instinct was to turn away. He looked as though he might have been drinking, the last thing in the world she needed tonight. He wobbled awkwardly, as if he were on stilts.

Better to avoid the question than to offend him. Whoever it was, she didn't know him, and she simply didn't want to dance.

At the last minute, though, something indefinable about the man stopped her.

She squinted, bewildered. The cap, which was far too large for the man's head, said *Two Wings: Todd,* but it definitely wasn't Todd who wore it.

So who was it?

He came closer, and she finally could make

out features. The smiling, silly, mustached face that peeked out from under that cap belonged to...

She looked again, disbelieving.

The mustache was clearly fake, probably drawn with a fat black marker.

But the smiling, freckled face was Harry's.

Harry? Harry was only about three feet tall. This man was more like...six feet. Taller than she was. Almost as tall as Logan.

He lurched closer still, and she looked again. The sneakered feet below the too-long, strangely lumpy coat belonged to Sean.

"Mrs. Archer?" Harry's voice was pitched artificially low, as husky as a baby bullfrog. He leaned forward, jeopardizing his big brother's balance, and she heard the muffled sound of Sean's voice saying, "Be still, darn it!"

"Yes?" She smiled at the mysterious stranger, the only "man" in the world she would never turn down.

"Umm... I'd like the honor..." Harry frowned, clearly forgetting his lines. "Mrs. Archer, would you like to dance?"

He held out his small hands, from which the coat's arms comically dangled.

Out of the corner of her eye, she saw the people closest to them slow down, then stop dancing altogether so that they could watch. Harry kept swiveling his head to the left, and when Nora glanced in that direction she saw Logan nodding and gesturing, reminding Harry what to do.

Somewhere, Evelyn was probably watching, too, but Nora didn't care about her at all.

"I'd be honored, sir," she said in her most ladylike voice. Harry beamed, clearly thrilled that he hadn't messed anything up.

The band was playing "Bye Bye Blackbird," for the third time already tonight. Their repertoire of animal songs was a bit limited.

But no one minded that, least of all Nora. She took Harry's hands, and they began to dance.

It was an ungainly waltz, never in time to the music, always on the edge of tumbling disaster. Sean, half-blind as he tried to see between the coat buttons, stepped on her feet a dozen times. Over and over, Harry threatened to slip from his perch on Sean's shoulders, and the boys would fuss at each other in loud whispers they seemed to believe Nora was unable to hear.

Even so, it was the most beautiful dance of her life. And when it was over, as she kissed Harry's mustached face, then leaned down to part the trench coat and plant another on Sean's flushed and perspiring cheek, the watching crowd erupted into spontaneous applause.

She knew why they clapped. Whether they were Harrison's friends, or Nora's, they applauded to show that they understood how difficult the past six months had been for this cruelly truncated family.

They clapped to say the struggle had not gone unnoticed, and they cared.

Harry, of course, was too young to comprehend any of that. He thought he was a star, and he soaked up the attention. Bowing clumsily to his audience, he jiggled his eyebrows and twisted his mouth into contorted shapes, trying to make his mustache move.

"Get down, dork," Sean grumbled. "You're breaking my neck."

Harry ignored the request. He fixed his bright eyes on Nora. "It's Mr. Logan's coat. He drew my mustache, too. We fooled you, didn't we, Mom? We did really good."

She nodded, and her eyes misted up, blurring his sweet face.

"You sure did, honey," she said. "You did great."

By ten o'clock, people started to trickle off. As Logan stood between the gift shop and the parking lot saying his goodbyes, he was exhausted, but deeply content.

His goal today had been to introduce Two Wings to Eastcreek, so that the community would welcome and support the work he wanted to do.

He was pretty sure he'd succeeded. The volunteer sign-up sheet overflowed with names, and extras had been scribbled in the margins. The donation box was packed to the gills, with several gifts handed to him directly, as well as pledges of many more to come.

Enthusiasm was at its peak right now, of course, and interest would undoubtedly fade over time. But he felt confident that enough goodwill would remain to keep the sanctuary going.

"Thank you, Logan." Jenny Wilcox, the pastor's wife, kissed his cheek. Her husband waved as he lugged three bags of books and toys from the gift shop. "Remember, I want you to talk to our Wednesday Women's Club. Some of them couldn't come tonight, and they will be so disappointed when they hear how wonderful it was."

"You bet," Logan said. "Any time."

As he made similar promises to one departing guest after another, the whole thing felt a little like a dream. Eighteen months ago, this project had seemed so remote, ambitious to the point of insanity. How could he ever create the income stream—no, income *flood*—a sanctuary needed? Just acquiring the state and federal permits was a gauntlet of red tape and planning and keeping the permits required gaining entrée to enough groups to satisfy his education requirements.

So much to worry about. So many hurdles to jump.

Yet somehow he'd managed to get Two Wings safely launched.

And now he wanted a nap.

He stifled a yawn as he said goodbye to Missy Snowdon, a busty young divorcée who had pressed a generous check into the palm of his hand earlier tonight while they were dancing.

He had a sneaking suspicion that Missy hoped she was buying a date with her money. He'd tried to set her straight—he didn't need cash *that* bad. But she struck him as the stubborn type, like Max the hawk—creatures who willfully ignored the bits of reality that didn't please them.

Finally, Missy headed to her car, a hot, low-

slung red convertible that screamed desperation, and Logan breathed a sigh of relief.

"Watch out for that one," Nora said, coming
up beside him as the convertible growled out of
the parking lot. "As predators go, Missy Snowdon is definitely at the top of the food chain."

"Oh, yeah?" He chuckled. "Like, maybe, a
broad-winged hawk?"

Nora smiled. "Exactly like a broad-winged
hawk. And every man she meets is a mouse."

"Thanks for the warning. I promise to be
careful." He glanced around. "Where are the
boys?"

"They're in the gift shop. I told them they
could each buy any one thing they wanted."
She groaned happily. "I must have been crazy.
Harry will probably fall in love with one of the
ninety-nine-cent finger puppets, but Sean is already considering that soapstone owl. I think
it costs about five hundred dollars."

Logan couldn't take his eyes off her. She
stood in a circle of light from one of the quaint
black carriage lamps that illuminated the sidewalk. Though she must be nearly as tired as
he was, her eyes were sparkling, and her smile
was warm and soft.

He could almost believe she was the one

who cast the glow. He hadn't ever seen her look quite this...hopeful.

He hoped that he—or at least Two Wings—had been a part of that.

"Well, I offer a pretty good volunteer discount," he said. "For you, I'm thinking maybe...a hundred percent."

She laughed. "Wow. Mr. Generosity. That check Missy Snowdon gave you must have been huge. Be careful you don't get tangled up in the strings she attached, though. I hear they lead straight to her red-velvet bedroom."

Logan started to respond with something teasing, but just then he noticed a car pulling into the parking lot. That was odd. No one should be arriving at this hour. The traffic was all headed in the other direction, out of the sanctuary and into the night.

Was a parent coming to pick up a teen? A husband ferrying home his wife?

But he didn't think so. Some sixth sense prickled as the car drew closer. Some instinct he'd picked up from the birds, maybe, that alerted him to an unidentified danger floating toward him on the currents of the darkness.

The car pulled into the first space. The engine stopped, the lights flicked off. And then, two people climbed out.

He held his breath, waiting to see if anyone else emerged. But it was just the two of them, just the tall, dark-haired man and the beautiful blonde woman.

His muscles tightened. A pulse beat in his temple.

"Oh, my God," he said under his breath.

Nora misunderstood. "Oh, I'm just kidding with you," she said. "Missy Snowdon isn't really anything to worry about. She—"

"No." He shook his head. "It's not that. It's… it's Rebecca."

Nora peered toward the parking lot, where the arriving couple strolled easily toward them, hand in hand.

"Who is Rebecca?"

"Rebecca is my ex-wife," he said.

"Oh." Nora put her hand on his arm, apparently without even realizing it. "And that man with her. Is he…"

Logan had to laugh at his own idiocy. He should have mentioned this earlier. A week ago. A month ago. It would have been so easy to bring it up casually, to get the information out as if it were no big deal.

Now he'd lost his chance to pretend he didn't care.

"That man is Benjamin Cathcart. Rebecca's new husband."

Nora inhaled sharply. "Cathcart?"

The couple had almost reached the sidewalk. He was going to have to pull himself together. He'd known this day would come. He'd only moved to Texas, not the moon, and eventually Ben and Becca were going to want to make an overture. Mend a fence.

Heal a family.

"That's right," he said. "Rebecca is married to my brother."

Chapter Thirteen

Nora hadn't even realized Logan had an ex-wife.

And now, just twenty-four hours after meeting Rebecca Cathcart for the first time, Nora found herself sitting across the table from her, making small talk.

Or trying to.

When she'd called Logan, earlier this afternoon, ostensibly to talk about picking up the decorations from the amphitheater but actually to see how he was doing, he'd impulsively invited her to dinner.

She hadn't been sure exactly what his motives were. He sounded as if he'd even surprised himself with the words. She'd said yes because she had a feeling he might need someone there as a buffer.

And because she wanted to see him again.

So she'd said yes, though it was a Sunday night, and she had to get an extra babysitter, to backstop Milly, who obviously wasn't up to the task of keeping Sean in line...or even in the house.

"A buffer" wasn't precisely a date, but... what was it? Nora wasn't sure how to dress or act. In an attack of girly insecurity she hadn't experienced since high school, she spent way too much time picking out her clothes. And yet, when she arrived at Logan's house she realized she'd made every possible mistake.

She'd chosen a floral wraparound silk dress and green sandals, which had seemed like comfortable spring casual in her mirror at home. Here, in Logan's simple cottage, with its masculine simplicity, book-lined walls and half-furnished rooms, the outfit looked prissy and ridiculous.

Rebecca Cathcart answered the door barefoot and smiling, and immediately Nora felt embarrassingly overdone.

"Nora!" Rebecca leaned in to kiss her cheek, as if they were already friends. "I've heard so much about you and your boys. Come on in. Logan and Ben are in the kitchen, ruining dinner. I hope you're not hungry."

Nora wanted to hate her. She didn't know the details of the crazy triangle, but the basic outline was damning enough. This woman had been married to Logan, and now she was married to his brother.

Even worse, Rebecca had been born so beautiful she had to play it down to make it work. Her hair was long, shining and as blonde as new corn. Her eyes were summer-sky blue, her lips full and pink, her body dramatic and graceful.

But she appeared charmingly indifferent to all that. Her hair was clipped away from her face in an off-center twist, and if she wore makeup it was too subtle to see. She was dressed simply but elegantly. A pair of black slacks and a royal blue fitted cotton shirt, tail out and sleeves rolled up to the elbow.

She looked like exactly what Logan had told Nora she was: a twenty-seven-year-old junior partner in a high-powered law firm, relaxing with her family. Unclip the hair, throw on an Armani jacket, and Rebecca could head straight for the courtroom, destined to win every case.

They had wandered into the kitchen, which was like the rest of the house, spare and masculine. Few frills, but everything was practical and high quality.

Ben was an older, more urbane version of Logan. Same intense blue eyes, rugged bone structure, thick, dark hair. Tall, broad-shouldered. A little less reserved, a little more fluid with the small talk, but basically the same model.

It was almost too much virility and charisma for one little cottage to hold.

The meal had been less awkward than she'd feared. The couple had been in Austin, she learned, at a legal conference. They'd decided that, since they were so close to Eastcreek, they would stop by for a surprise visit.

Logan smiled when they described their decision, as if it were delightful to see them. Everyone was trying very hard, she could tell, to cover over any cracks in the family bond.

But Nora had heard the hollow horror in his voice when he first glimpsed them and said, "Oh, my God."

Besides, she wasn't a fool. She knew the cracks had to be there. Chasms, in fact.

Two brothers. One wife. No way that story didn't involve a lot of pain.

Suddenly Nora understood why Logan had given up law. Why he'd left Maine, where, she'd learned tonight, the Cathcarts had lived for two hundred years.

Why he preferred the company of silent, watchful birds to the company of his fellow man.

"So you and Logan are dating?" Rebecca peeled a grape casually, as if the question weren't important, but her voice was pitched deliberately low. She obviously didn't want the men, who were energetically discussing the latest Supreme Court nominee, to overhear.

Nora hesitated. She wasn't sure what Logan had told them. Maybe he wanted Ben and Rebecca to believe he had a girlfriend.

"Well," she said, perfectly prepared to lie, if she could be certain lying was required. At its heart, it wouldn't even be a falsehood. If Rebecca wanted to know whether other women desired her ex-husband, whether he had chances to love and be loved, the answer was unequivocally yes.

Half the women in Eastcreek were a little bit in love with him. Why, last night, even fifty-year-old happily married Jenny Wilcox had broken the bank buying things at the gift shop, just to support his cause.

Still…

What was the right answer? She glanced at Logan, wishing she knew for sure.

"I'm sorry." Rebecca smiled apologetically at Nora. "I can't stop being a lawyer, I guess. Let me rephrase. I *hope* you and Logan are dating. You seem very close. It would mean a lot, to know that he was happy."

Nora felt herself bristling. Though Rebecca's tone had been gentle and sincere, wasn't it a little late for her to be worrying about Logan's happiness? And wasn't it a little self-serving? If Logan had indeed found another woman to love, did that let Rebecca off the hook? Did it absolve her of the sin of breaking his heart?

Nora glanced again at Logan, who was laughing at something Ben had said. He didn't laugh as often as Ben, or chatter as easily. He wasn't as slick or glib. He was just slightly more real, more vulnerable, more intense.

And massively more desirable. She couldn't imagine any woman choosing the older brother over the younger one. But of course she didn't know the whole story. She probably never would, and so she had no license to judge.

She returned her gaze to Rebecca.

"Right now, Two Wings takes all the time and energy Logan has," she said, deciding to be honest. She couldn't really imagine Logan lowering himself to lie about their relationship. "And I have two children who need mine." She smiled. "But all the same, Two Wings has come to mean a great deal to me."

Rebecca's gaze was searching, sharp, as if she were calculating her chances of eliciting anything more definitive. But, after a couple of seconds, she relaxed, apparently satisfied with what she found in Nora's face.

"Well, good, then," she said finally. "I'm very glad to hear it."

She took one last sip of her white wine. Tossing her napkin onto the table beside her plate to show the serious talk was over, she leaned back in her chair and smiled warmly at Nora.

"Now," she said, "tell me all about your boys."

"Thanks for tonight," Logan said as he walked Nora to her car an hour later. "I'm really glad you were able to come."

Actually, that was a colossal understatement. All day, he'd been dreading this dinner. He probably would have called it off if Nora had said no.

And calling it off would have been a mistake. Because he'd learned something very important tonight, as he sat across the table from his ex-wife and his brother, watching them struggle with their worry and their guilt.

He'd learned that somehow, sometime over the past eighteen months, he'd found his way out of the woods.

He was no longer even the least bit in love with Rebecca.

"I had a terrific time," Nora said. "I'm sorry I have to leave, but I promised the sitter I'd be back by eleven. She has school tomorrow."

The dinner had run much longer than he'd expected. The full moon was low in the sky, just barely clearing the treetops, and the crickets and frogs had gone silent. Nora would have to hurry to make it home by the appointed hour.

But neither one of them picked up the pace. Her car was only a few yards away, gleaming in the moonlight, and they clearly wanted to stretch the distance as far as they could, prolonging their few moments alone.

"Rebecca is very nice," Nora said hesitantly. "And your brother is charming."

"They're good people," he said.

He wished he could stop there, but he knew he owed her more. He'd brought her into this by asking her to come. "It's been a rough adjustment for all of us, but they're doing the best they can. They want to move past it, so that we can be family again."

They had reached her car. She put her fingers on the door handle, but she didn't pull it open. She leaned her hip against the side of the car, and turned her soft gaze his way.

"It's a lot for them to ask," she said with a staunch loyalty that was unexpectedly soothing. "To expect you to forgive them…"

"No." He couldn't bask in her compassion while allowing her to unfairly demonize Rebecca and Ben. "It wasn't like that, Nora. There's nothing to forgive."

He moved a few inches closer. He had no reason to worry about privacy. Rebecca and Ben, still inside the cottage, couldn't see the driveway from any of the windows. The solid stone-and-wood structure was practically soundproof. They couldn't hear anything spoken out here.

He had no reason. He just wanted to be close to her.

"It wasn't Rebecca's fault," he said. "She tried desperately to make it work. Our marriage failed because of me."

"I don't believe it." Nora frowned. "Nothing's that one-sided."

He shook his head. "It's true. I was a terrible husband. We married very young, and everything was okay for a while. Then…we hit some serious problems."

What a euphemism. Serious problems…

He wanted to be honest, but he just couldn't share everything, not even with Nora. "When things went wrong, I withdrew. Unfortunately, that's how I've always dealt with my emotions. But Rebecca was different. She…she needed someone to talk to."

"And that someone was your *brother?*"

He heard the indignation in Nora's voice, and he had to smile. She was so angry on his behalf, even all this time later.

So different from Logan himself. Had he ever, even once, allowed himself to experience any normal, honest emotions about what happened?

Probably not. By the time Rebecca divorced him, four months after Danny's death, Logan was already numb, already deep in the denial that had been his refuge for so long. The ache of losing her was distant, as if it were happening to someone else.

When she and Ben had come to him, a short six weeks later, and told him they were going to be married, he was shocked, just like everybody else.

As he sat there, watching the two people he loved most in the world pale and begging his forgiveness, on some level he was aware that he'd been betrayed.

But it had made very little difference to him. A poet once said that after the first death there is no other. That was true. He'd absorbed that blow, too, without really feeling it. He'd been civilized, understanding. He'd stayed in the firm with Ben, prepared to ride it out.

But when he learned that Rebecca was pregnant, he didn't think, didn't feel, didn't try to overcome. He'd been like an animal, programmed for fight or flight.

He'd chosen flight. He'd packed his bags that night and moved as far away from Maine as he could get. First to Florida for just over a year, then here.

He'd never seen his niece, Chloe. And he hoped he never would.

"Rebecca is happy with Ben," he said. "He is perfect for her. He gives her what she needs. And he loves her very much."

Nora's looked at him for a long moment. "And what about you?"

He tilted his head. "What about me?"

"Do you love her, too?"

Her voice was so somber. The cool night breeze was playing with her hair, tickling it across her cheeks. He reached out and gently tucked it behind her ear.

"No," he said quietly. "Not anymore. I probably haven't loved Rebecca for a long, long time."

She touched her cheek where his fingers had been. "Probably?"

"Well, that's one of the drawbacks of closing off your emotions. Sometimes you can't tell the difference between ignoring your feelings and having no feelings to ignore."

She looked pensive, her face pale in the moonlight, her eyes dark as they scanned his face. He had to fight the urge to touch her again. Her cheek, her hair, her hand. Any part of her.

Every part of her.

He put his hands in his pockets.

"Which one is it with me, Logan?" Her voice was breathy, as if she couldn't get quite enough air. "Are you ignoring how you feel? Or is there nothing to ignore?"

He shook his head. "Neither one. I'm lying

awake at night, warring with myself. Trying to think of an excuse to see you. Trying to stop myself from seeing you."

"Why? Why must there be war?"

"Because we don't want the same things. You want a husband and a father for your boys."

"That's ridiculous. I have no thoughts of marrying again, and—"

"Not yet, maybe. But ultimately, that's the only relationship you'd settle for. Even if you would consider anything less, you are in no position to have a hot, short-term fling, and you know it."

"I—" She hesitated, unable to finish the protest.

"Right. You'd never do it. Damn it, Nora, you nearly lost your mind when you thought Sean had simply seen you kissing me."

She looked away, and he knew she recognized the truth of his words.

"You don't want anything short of happily ever after. And that's fine. It's just that I don't believe in that fairy tale anymore. Believe me, I've already tried True Love, complete with hot sex, solemn vows and—"

He broke off. He'd been about to say complete with hot sex, solemn vows and a little blue crib.

"And it led to pure hell, for everyone involved."

Chapter Fourteen

By Friday, when Ben and Rebecca had been in town six days, Logan had to admit that some of the strangeness had finally worn off.

They were all probably fairly surprised that the reunion was progressing so smoothly. Ben and Rebecca had arranged for extra time off, and Logan's parents had apparently been happy to keep Chloe, Ben and Rebecca's little girl, for as long as they were needed.

Ben and Rebecca weren't actually sleeping at his place. The cottage was too small for that, with only one bedroom. But they stayed close by, at a hotel in downtown Eastcreek, and the three of them spent at least some time together every day.

Both Ben and Rebecca seemed impressed by the sanctuary, which was a relief. Logan knew that everyone in the family believed he'd made a terrible mistake in giving up law. He hoped they'd spread the word back home, where his parents were still writing weekly e-mails assuring him that his place in the firm was still open.

He wasn't going back to that career. He might have fled to Texas impulsively, just trying to escape, but along the way he'd found his calling.

The sooner everyone accepted that, the better.

When they reached Friday afternoon without any uncomfortable scenes or unwelcome heart-to-heart talks, Logan actually began to relax. Ben and Rebecca planned to return to Maine early Saturday morning, just about twelve hours from now. This dinner at his place would be their last get-together.

He had made it. It looked, thank God, as if they might come through this crucible unscathed.

Really?

Showed how dumb a man could be.

He should have known better than to start congratulating himself early. Fate loved to smack around anyone who got a little too smug.

They'd just finished a big pot of Rebecca's famous veggie stew, Ben's perfectly chosen wine and Logan's store-bought crusty rolls, when someone knocked on his front door. He wasn't expecting anyone, but his hopes took a little bounce, anyhow. He hadn't seen Nora or Sean all week, and he missed them more than he liked to admit.

Maybe they missed him, too. Maybe they'd invented some excuse to visit.

He had absolutely no reason to think so, except that he wanted it to be true. When he and Nora had parted Sunday night, it had been with the understanding that they needed to back away. At least for a while. At least until Sean settled down. Until the sexual tension eased up enough to let them breathe.

Still, like a fool, by the time he got to the door, he almost had himself convinced Nora would be standing there.

He pulled it open. The welcoming smile died on his face.

It was not Nora.

It was, though it took his stunned brain a

second or two to fully process it, his parents, who should have been in Maine.

And, standing beside his mother, holding her hand, stood an adorable, sleepy little girl. Not yet two years old, with dewy blue eyes and wispy hair as blond as Rebecca's.

"Hello, son," his father said.

"Dad?"

Logan sensed movement behind him, and realized that Ben and Rebecca had come to the door. As he glanced over his shoulder, he realized that neither of them looked the least bit surprised.

"Mommy," the little girl called out, her sleepy eyes widening with delight. "Mommy, I missed you!"

Rebecca moved forward eagerly and scooped her daughter into her arms. Stroking the satiny hair, she turned around and gave Logan a tremulous, apprehensive smile.

"I'm sorry," she said. "Ben… Ben thought it was time."

Goddamn it.

He had been set up.

He ought to be furious. He ought to toss them all out of his house. What right had they to intrude on the life he'd built so carefully?

What right to spring a hidden, steel-jawed trap, with a little girl as bait?

And yet, he found that he couldn't give voice to that fury. Now that Rebecca's daughter was a living child, and not just an idea, anger was no longer uppermost in his emotions.

This little girl, whose curious eyes peeked at him from under a fringe of feathery lashes, was not merely a symbol of betrayal, or even a reminder of loss.

She was his niece. She was his flesh and blood.

And she was completely innocent. She couldn't know that, simply by having her mother's hair, and the round, blue Cathcart eyes, she reminded him wrenchingly of Danny, the half brother she would never meet.

None of this dreadful, complicated mess was her fault.

In the end, his heart didn't consult his brain. It simply opened and accepted her, in spite of the inevitable pain.

"Hi, Chloe," he said. He bent down, so that he would be on her level, and she could see that they shared the same blue eyes. "It's nice to finally meet you. I'm your Uncle Logan."

Ordinarily, eleven o'clock on a Friday night found Nora immersed in a long, luxurious bubble bath, her celebration of an evening off from mother-duty. After the bath, she usually treated herself to a glass of wine and a good book. If she was feeling particularly frisky, she might even go down to Milly's room and play gin rummy till midnight.

Yeah, she was a wild woman, all right.

But because some thorny decisions about how to use a patch of land needed to be made immediately, Nora's weekly meeting with the foreman had run late. Instead of pampering herself as the clock struck eleven, she was walking Dusty out to his car.

The moon was still almost full, clearly illuminating the long, wide oyster-shell drive that led up to the hacienda. Because the round disc was so bright, almost like a silver sun, she saw the glossy black Mercedes coming up the hill long before she heard it.

How strange…at this time of night. She recognized the sports car. It belonged to Ben and Rebecca Cathcart.

She wondered what they were doing at the Bull's Eye. Could Logan be with them?

"Want me to wait here awhile?" Dusty, who had loved Harrison and felt a duty to offer his protection to Harrison's widow, eyed the incoming car suspiciously. "I'm not in a hurry."

"No, that's fine," she said, smiling her thanks. "I know who it is. I'll be fine."

He dawdled anyhow, pretending to fumble with his keys, so that he was still within earshot when the Mercedes finally pulled up in front of the fountain.

When Rebecca Cathcart emerged from the passenger's side, looking delicate and gorgeous in the moonlight, Dusty started his truck's motor. He obviously couldn't imagine such a vision of femininity being a threat to anyone.

"Hi," Rebecca said, her voice slightly stilted as she walked toward Nora. "I'm glad you're still awake. We hated to come so late, but..."

She glanced back toward the car, where Ben presumably waited behind the wheel. "We really thought we should talk to you before we go back home. We fly out first thing in the morning."

"All right." Nora gestured toward the front door. "Would you like to come in?"

"Thanks, no. Chloe is already asleep in her car seat. This won't take long. It's just that—" She sighed, as if annoyed with herself. "Darn it, I'm just going to come out and say it. I don't know where things stand between you and Logan. But this has been a very difficult night for him. I think... I think he needs you."

Nora was, quite literally, speechless. Though she'd been over at Two Wings several times during the week, she hadn't seen Logan. She'd spent most of her time helping Vic, whose wife was four days beyond her due date with no signs of impending labor, leaving him so distraught he could hardly focus.

But she occasionally heard other workers talking about Logan. The word was that he, Rebecca and Ben were having a lovely family reunion. She'd been happy for him.

So what had gone wrong?

And who was Chloe?

"I know my coming here is a risk." Rebecca raised her hands, palms up, indicating her vulnerability. "I suspect you don't like me much. And, of course, I could be completely wrong about your feelings for him."

Nora frowned. She didn't dislike Rebecca, exactly. But it was hard to trust a woman who had done what this woman did. Logan might have chivalrously accepted all the blame, but Nora knew it took two people to destroy a marriage.

And, in her opinion, it took an extremely self-absorbed, cold-hearted woman to leap from one brother's bed to another's.

"Actually," Nora said, deciding to be as blunt

as Rebecca had been, "your only error is thinking I would discuss my feelings, or lack of them, with you. Frankly, I'm not sure I understand what your stake is in this situation."

Rebecca took the rebuff well. She nodded, as if she fully appreciated Nora's position. "That's simple enough. My stake is that I love him."

Nora didn't respond in words. But she assumed her skeptical expression was answer enough.

"I really do," Rebecca said. "But it's not important whether you believe me. I don't want you to discuss your feelings with me. I don't even want you to discuss them with Logan. I just want you to listen."

"Listen? To you?"

"No, to him. I have a feeling he may, for once in his life, be ready to open up to someone. And I think that someone is you."

Logan had been working in the amphitheater for at least two hours, maybe three. To get ready for the open house, they'd made all the public areas perfect, but the backstage storage areas were still a mess.

He'd been tearing out rotten wood and drywall until his shoulders burned. The halogen work lights he'd set up transformed night to day, and he had no idea what time it really was.

All he knew was that he hadn't worked long enough, or hard enough, to drain the tension out of his system. If he tried to go to bed now, he'd never sleep. He'd just lie there, opening his memories one by one, like so many Pandora's boxes, until he drove himself insane.

So, though he was covered in sweat and plaster, and the windowless rooms were as hot as the inside of a volcano, he was going to keep at it, till dawn if necessary.

He dragged off his sticky shirt, then twisted the nozzle on the outside of the amphitheater to turn on the hose.

Bending at the waist, he let the water pour over him from head to toe. It might soak his hair and his jeans, but at least it cooled him down and washed away some of the grit and grime. He shook his head, spraying water everywhere, then scraped his hair back from his face.

Now where had he put the crowbar? He would pull down this whole place, plank by plank, if that was what it took to make the memories of Danny go back where they belonged.

"Logan?"

The voice seemed to be coming from the concrete rows of seating that fanned out from the stage, up the natural bowl of land into which the amphitheater had been carved. He looked, but his halogen-blinded eyes could make nothing out of the darkness.

"Logan, it's me." Her footsteps were soft on the grassy earth between the seats. "It's Nora. Are you there?"

God, he wished she hadn't come. It didn't matter whether she was here because she needed him, or because she believed he needed her.

Whatever she wanted, he couldn't give it to her.

He was too frayed, too raw, too close to the edge. He didn't trust himself. He didn't have the self-control tonight. He couldn't guarantee he'd do the right thing. He was no longer even sure what the right thing was.

Finally her form differentiated itself from the other shadows beyond his lights. She'd made her way onto the stage, obviously following the illumination.

He had to say something. Surely he wasn't so far gone that he could only stand here, frozen by the sound of her voice.

"I'm in the back, Nora," he said. But his voice sounded strained. "In the storage room."

He hadn't realized what he must look like, until he saw the shock on her face. And then he could imagine it all too clearly. He must look like a madman. Half-naked, gleaming with sweat, hair dripping into his forehead, a jagged plank in his hands, rubble all around him.

"Oh, Logan," she breathed. She moved quickly to him and put her palm against his wet, flushed cheek. "What is it? What happened?"

He stepped back. "Nothing happened."

He ran both hands through his hair, trying to stop the rivulets of hose water. "I've been tearing out some old wood. It's late, Nora. What are you doing here?"

"I'm looking for you." Her face was as somber, as worried as he'd ever seen it look, even when Sean was at his worst. "Logan, please. Tell me what happened."

Tell her?

The hell he would.

And yet…it startled him, the sudden violent urge he felt to do exactly that.

"Nothing happened," he repeated, but it felt rote, strangely desperate, the way a prisoner might issue denial after denial under interrogation, always fearing that on the next round he might crack. "Nora, go home. Please. Just go home."

"I can't," she said. "I'm worried about you. You look sick. Have you hurt yourself?"

"I'm fine. I just need to be alone." He rubbed his hand over his eyes. The lights were beginning to give him a headache. "Please. Go. We can talk tomorrow."

"I can't," she said. She almost sounded sorry, as if she wished she could do as he asked but it just wasn't possible. Her resolve sounded much more absolute than his, and he wondered why she cared so much.

Even if it was obvious he was sinking, why didn't she just cut him loose?

"Logan, who is Chloe?"

He knew, then, what had happened. Rebecca had called her, and asked her to come by and check on him. So apparently his show of emotional composure, his stoic "time heals all wounds" charade, hadn't fooled anyone. They all knew what seeing Chloe had really done to him.

"Chloe is Rebecca's daughter," he said. He wasn't sure why he sounded angry. He wasn't angry, and yet there it was, that harsh, serrated edge at the underside of his voice. "Rebecca and Ben have a daughter. I have a niece. I knew about her, of course. But I hadn't met her, until tonight."

Nora's eyes widened. "How old is she?"

"Eighteen months."

Nora bit her lower lip, and he could almost see the mental calculations. She began to speak, but he stopped her.

"Don't ask," he said. "The answer is no. Chloe was not conceived while Rebecca was still married to me. No matter what you think, Nora, Rebecca isn't the bad guy here. I am." He tossed the rotten board onto the pile in the corner. "*I am.* I don't know why you can't bring yourself to believe that."

Her face looked very pale and small in the bright lights.

"I don't know, either," she said with a simple candor. "I just can't. Maybe it's because I haven't seen a moment's cruelty from you, in the whole time I've known you. Not to me, not to the birds, not even to Sean."

"Marriage is different. It's up close, and it's ugly. It requires things I wasn't prepared to give. Especially when our son…"

Perversely, now, he wanted her to interrupt him. Wanted her to push, to press for more so that his instinct to resist would kick in, and stop him.

But she didn't say a word. She watched him with those round, gleaming eyes, and waited.

"Especially after our son... Danny."

Shut up, shut up, he commanded himself. But now that he'd started, he didn't seem to be able to stop.

"Especially after Danny died."

"Oh, my God. Logan." Nora took a step toward him, then checked herself. "I didn't know. Your son...?"

And suddenly, he knew what he'd really been doing out here with the crowbar, and the sweat and the pain. He'd been tearing down the final pieces of the barricade he'd built around this memory.

Over the past few weeks, it had begun to weaken. The chinks became fissures, the fissures became a breach. And finally, tonight, it was as if the defenses simply crumbled, and the long-repressed emotions flooded through.

He backed up, instinctively, as if he could avoid the torrent. When the real wall of the storage room hit his back, he leaned against it, and accepted that there was no escape.

"What happened?" Her question was soft, as if she knew she probed an open wound.

"An accident," he said. "One of those terrible, senseless combinations of mistakes that strike out of the blue. One of those moments when, if anyone involved had done one single thing differently, the danger would have passed us by."

He didn't have to wonder whether she understood that. By all accounts, the fire that had killed Harrison's first son, Paul, had been one of those cruel mistakes. It had damaged so many lives, including hers.

And maybe it wasn't finished working its evil. Sean, too, stood poised to become its victim.

"What happened?" The repeated question didn't sound intrusive. It sounded stunned.

It was an almost unanswerable question. What moment, what decision, had been the trailhead, leading inexorably to disaster?

"I was supposed to pick Danny up from nursery school that day. I didn't want to. Can you believe that? But Rebecca and I were always so busy. Always another case to argue, another precedent to research, another client to meet. We argued, that day, about who would have to pick him up. I lost."

He waited for her to say what everyone had said back then. It wasn't his fault. He shouldn't blame himself. Juggling a career and children was difficult, and even the best parents wore out and lost patience sometimes.

But she didn't say any of those things. She looked almost as if she understood. Could she? Could her intuition tell her what he would always believe, on some deep, irrational level?

He'd always believe he'd lost the most miraculous thing in his life simply because he failed to appreciate how lucky he was.

"My meeting ran long. Maybe that was deliberate. Passive-aggressive, proving to Rebecca that we needed to hire someone to chauffeur Danny around. Or maybe I really couldn't help it. At any rate, I was late."

How clearly he could see it, even now. The familiar, boring pick-up line in front of the school. The teachers standing beneath the overhang, waiting for the right car, popping the children in, making sure they remembered their blue-macaroni artwork and their red superhero lunchboxes. Smiles and waves, then the next towheaded child slipped into his mommy's car like bread into a toaster.

"But by the time I got there, Danny was the only child left. The teacher was frustrated, distracted, trying to phone me. I'd been late so many times before."

All those meetings, all those cups of coffee and empty words. How could he ever have thought they were more important than listening to Danny chatter about Mrs. Weickel's classroom hamster?

"He was so happy to spot my car. He…the teacher wasn't holding his hand. He smiled when he saw me." Logan looked at Nora, knowing that was irrelevant. But somehow it was almost unbearable, the memory of that beaming smile.

"Then he ran into the street."

"Oh, no." Nora's simple exhalation was filled with pain. "Oh, Logan, no."

He shut his eyes. Here it was again. The infinite looping of the impossible, soul-splitting moment when Danny had come dashing out, into the path of the impatient teenaged driver who decided, in that fateful millisecond, to try to shoot past Logan's slowing car.

In the first days after Danny's death, that image was the only information Logan's brain would process. He'd tried to talk, but no words could make it past the endlessly repeating horror. He'd tried to eat, but nothing would go down. He'd tried to make decisions, but nothing made any sense.

He'd wondered if someone would come, finally, and take him away to a place where he could just sit quietly, watching the mental pictures, until his life was over, too. But no one did. And so he had begun to build the barricade.

Denial, Rebecca called it, as she begged him to talk to her, to cry like a normal person. To look at Danny's pictures, to bare his soul to the grief counselor.

But he called it survival.

Whatever name you gave it, that barrier had worked, for almost four years. It had allowed him to live among normal people, just as if he were one of them.

But the barricade was in ruins now. He wasn't even sure what, or who, had been the catalyst. Was it Chloe? Nora? Sean?

Maybe all of them.

Or perhaps it had been his own half-smothered life force, determined to bust free at any price.

All he knew for sure was that, for better or worse, there was no going back now.

Chapter Fifteen

Nora had no idea what to say.

It was so easy to imagine being where Logan was tonight. What would have become of her life, if on one of those dangerous late-night escapades, something terrible had happened to Sean? Would anyone have been able to console her? Would any platitude, however heartfelt, make even a microscopic difference?

Of course not.

So, though her heart broke for him, she said nothing.

Instead, acting purely on instinct, she went up to him and put her palms against his bare, wet chest. Maybe a touch could do what words could not.

And oh, how long she'd wanted to touch him.

He made a low sound, and stiffened immediately. "No," he growled.

The intensity of his response shocked her. "What's wrong?"

"Don't romanticize this. I told you about Danny because I want you to know I meant what I said. My marriage failed because of me. Rebecca needed me, and I wasn't there for her. I wouldn't even let her talk about him."

"But—you're wrong," she said.

"I'm not. Rebecca turned to Ben because she was drowning in grief, and I didn't do a damn thing to save her."

She shook her head. "I mean you're wrong about me. I'm not romanticizing anything."

He glanced at her hands. "No? Then what are you doing?"

"I'm—I'm not sure," she said honestly. She hesitated, then let the words come out. "I think I'm asking you to make love to me."

He cursed under his breath. Gripping her shoulders, he held her at a few inches distance.

"Damn it, Nora. Are you offering me pity sex?" His face was so strained she almost didn't recognize him. "Could you possibly think I told you the story of my dead son to get you into bed?"

She almost laughed, the idea was so absurd. The physical chemistry between them had always been as dangerous as walking through an electrical storm.

"Of course not. I think you told me about Danny because you were tired of being alone with your grief." She felt his heart racing under her palm. "And that's the same reason I'm asking you to make love to me. I'm tired. I'm tired of being alone."

He kept his face hard, his muscles tight.

"We talked about this," he said. "We decided it would be a mistake. We have different needs."

"Not tonight." She smiled softly. "Tonight we both want exactly the same thing. We want not to be alone."

He shut his eyes tightly for a few seconds, as if looking inside himself for strength. She waited, letting herself drink in the rugged beauty of his face, his broad shoulders, his sculpted chest. A warm, slow, melting feeling began to seep through her, from her stomach to her knees. At the same time, in her neck and arms, her blood seemed to be moving faster, tingling in her veins.

The combination made her feel intensely alive, deeply female, hungry for something she'd almost forgotten existed.

But that wasn't really true. It *hadn't* ever existed, not for her. She had never ached like this inside, longing for a man's body to fill her. She'd never been so consumed with the need to feel his fingers, his lips against her skin. Never on fire with this kind of mindless, urgent passion.

She ought to be frightened. But she wasn't. Instead, she was deeply, profoundly grateful that it had come to her at last. She would not have wanted to grow old without knowing this.

She began to move her fingertips, stroking the damp skin of his collarbone. *Please,* she said with her fingers. *Please, let him be feeling it, too.*

"Nora." His eyes were open now, their blue shockingly intense in the glare of the work lights. "Nora, nothing has changed. If you give in to this, this temporary weakness, you'll hate yourself tomorrow."

"No." She shook her head, firm and slow. "I'll hate myself if I don't. I've waited my whole life to feel like this. I'm not afraid of facing tomorrow. I'm afraid of losing tonight."

His hands had never let go of her shoulders, as if his sanity depended on keeping her away even that little bit. But finally, they surrendered. As if against his will, they slid down her spine roughly, until they were pressed against the small of her back. Unconsciously, her body tilted into him, and she felt the hard proof of his desire pushing against his jeans.

Something lurched inside her, a quick spasm of longing that left her shivering and weak. She moved against him, wanting more.

He groaned. "If you're hoping I'll come through with some superhuman nobility at the last minute, you're making a mistake. I don't have any. Not tonight."

She lifted her face to his. "Then hurry, please, before I lose my mind. Make love to me."

With a dark sweep of passion, his arms closed around her. He spoke her name once more, and then his mouth claimed hers with a ferocity that swept all thought from its path.

The room seemed to swirl around her, and she feared her legs wouldn't hold her up much longer. Until those hot, hard lips touched hers, she hadn't begun to understand how much raging fire had been banked behind his stoic exterior.

Suddenly he pulled away, leaving her mouth thick and lost.

"Come," he said. He took her hand, and somehow they were out of the amphitheater, down the stairs and moving across the moonlit grass before she could even be sure what was happening.

The house was yards and yards away, and twice they had to stop, just so that they could kiss again, and feel again the heat of their arms around each other. Night birds hooted mournfully, the wind spoke to the trees, and she was melting. She didn't care about getting inside, or lying on cool sheets. She wanted him now.

But he kept moving, swift and confident through these grounds he knew so well, and finally they reached the cottage. They went in through the back, because it was closer, and then, miraculously, they were in his bedroom.

He kissed her again, and her breath came fast against his hard lips. Finally, it was going to happen. They might not make it to the bed, though they'd come so close. After all these weeks of iron control, he clearly had no patience left.

He dragged her silk panties down and tossed

them aside as if they were just more useless rubble. He gathered her skirt in his hands and raised it to her waist. He lifted one of her legs and wrapped it around his lean hips. Then with long, hard fingers he touched between her legs and found the pulsing heat that told him she was ready.

He was in total control of her body, and it was hot and wild and wonderful, but it was too much, and she was going to explode; she was going to fall apart in his hands if he didn't stop. She dug her nails into his shoulder, and made noises she'd never heard herself make.

"Wait," she whispered, forcing the words out around her panting breaths. She was fighting the fall, but he was making it impossible. How could he know exactly where the trigger was, how could he make this happen so fast?

She didn't want to begin like this. She reached down and ran her hand along the hard length of him. She wished she could tell him what she wanted, without being disloyal to Harrison's memory.

In ten years of marriage, she had never climaxed during the act of sex. But this time, she knew, would be different.

In every possible way, making love with Logan would be different.

And the biggest difference of all was...

Somehow, sometime over the past few weeks, she'd fallen deeply in love with this complex and wounded man.

It didn't seem possible, but she knew it was true. It was also a terrible mistake. He didn't love her. He didn't want commitment or complications. He wanted only this one night of oblivion, and the release that sex could bring.

She was going to get her heart broken, just as he'd warned her she would.

But she didn't care about that now.

Tomorrow, she would grapple with the hundreds of implications, large and small. Tomorrow, she would start learning to live with the heartache of unrequited love.

But tonight, she refused to be anything but glad that this beautiful chance had come to her.

Tonight, for the first time in her life, her hungry body and her lonely heart would belong to the same man.

And that was worth whatever followed.

When her cell phone rang, for a minute Nora didn't know where she was. She heard its muffled, tinny music, emanating from a distance, but where...?

She sat up in the semidarkness, and the soft

cotton sheets that had been covering her fell away. The cool air-conditioning blew against her bare skin, and with a sharp inhale she lay her forearm across her naked breast.

And suddenly remembered everything.

She pushed her tangled hair from her face and glanced around. She was in Logan's bedroom. They had—

They had just spent the past few hours making love.

Over and over, as if they refused to let a minute of this night, the only one they would have, be wasted. Over and over, he spun magic with his bare hands, coaxed her secret dreams from her body with his lips.

And then, though her heart would have come back endlessly for more, her body had finally given out. She must have fallen asleep.

Moonlight filtered through leafy oak branches and lay in dappled patterns on the bed. The illumination was dim, but it was enough to show her that Logan was no longer sleeping next to her. Instead, there was a square of white paper. On it, he'd written, in bold, black strokes, "Checking on Hank. Back ASAP. Maybe sooner."

Could he be the one calling? Did he need help in the sanctuary?

She scrambled out of bed, ignoring her nakedness, and hunted down her dress, which had ended up across the large, tweedy armchair in the corner. The phone must be in the pocket. After Rebecca's troubling visit, Nora had driven away from Bull's Eye with nothing but her driver's license, her car keys and her phone.

Everything was turned inside out, so she fumbled to find the opening to the pocket. When her fingers finally closed around the phone, she flipped it open with one finger and began speaking even before it reached her ear.

"Hello?"

"I know where you are, Nora."

The voice on the other end was so raspy, so deep with bitterness, that for a weird instant Nora didn't realize it was Evelyn.

When she did identify the voice, she had an irrational desire to laugh. Those words were so cliché, the universal code for menace.

I know where you are, and I saw what you did...

But the impulse lasted only a fraction of a second. Laughing at Evelyn was stupid, and if Nora hadn't still been drunk on the bubbling joy of being in Logan's arms, she wouldn't have considered it.

The Nora who had spent those incredible hours in that bed was afraid of nothing. Logan's lips had awakened her fairy-tale heart, and turned her soul to gold and fire.

But that Nora had slept, and she had awakened to the real world, where she was merely human.

"I know where you are," Evelyn repeated, "and I want you to come home this instant."

Foolishly, Nora picked up her dress and held it across herself, as if she needed privacy even from her sister-in-law's voice.

"Why would I do that?" She tried to sound firm but not inflammatory. "Why would I go home?"

But then she realized that Evelyn hadn't said "go" home. She'd said "come" home.

Nora's hand tightened on the phone. "Evelyn. Are you at Bull's Eye?"

"Yes."

"Why?"

"One of Ginger's puppies died in the night. Sean couldn't handle it. He insisted on being taken home to his mother. You can imagine my surprise when, at three in the morning, we arrived at Bull's Eye, but his mother was nowhere to be found."

"Is he all right now?"

"Of course he's not all right." Evelyn sounded disgusted. "I don't know what that therapist says he's doing with all the money he's stealing from you, but obviously it isn't working. The boy has no ability to handle death of any kind. He's in his room right now, weeping his heart out. I told him Harrison would be embarrassed to have a son who acts like a five-year-old girl—"

"You told him what?" Nora's temper erupted. "How dare you say such a thing? I never shame the boys for crying."

"Well, you weren't here, were you? *I was.* I'll say it one more time. Come home. I've invented a story to cover for you with the boys. I don't know if they believe it. When we saw you weren't here, Sean's first thought was that you might be with Cathcart. You can thank me for not bringing them over there in the flesh, so that they could see what a tramp their mother is."

A hundred furious retorts screamed through Nora's mind. But the time for words, kind or cruel, was over between the two of them.

And so, instead, she merely hung up the phone.

She pulled on her dress, then grabbed the

white square Logan had left on the pillow and prepared to add her own words at the bottom.

It was beautiful, she wanted to say. *It was magic.*

But instead she wrote the words she assumed he needed most to hear.

Don't worry. I understand that nothing has changed.

Chapter Sixteen

The meeting at Evelyn's lawyer's office seemed like a waste of time to Nora. What was there left to say?

The line had been drawn in the sand. Nora had no more concessions to make, no compromises to offer.

If Evelyn really tried to take the boys away from her, she'd find out exactly how badly she'd underestimated Nora all these years.

But Frederick Corrado, the attorney Jim Stilling had recommended, believed that Nora should make every effort to appear cooperative, in the hopes that they could still avoid a court hearing.

So she had put on a red dress, to show she didn't intend to be cowed into donning sack-cloth to prove her virtue, and arrived at East-creek's swankiest downtown office building ten minutes early.

Then she'd proceeded to spend a full half an hour pretending she didn't hear the thinly veiled insults in every sentence Evelyn uttered.

Even her conciliatory lawyer was starting to show his irritation. "Is Mrs. Gellner implying that Mr. Archer's will is somehow suspect?"

"No, of course not." Vince Begetti, Evelyn's lawyer, looked miserable.

As well he should. He'd been a guest at Bull's Eye a hundred times, and he knew damn well Nora had been a good wife and mother.

She'd even been a good sister-in-law, which was more than anyone could say about Evelyn.

"But there's some indication," Vince continued, "that, by the time Harrison died, his judgment—"

Corrado, her lawyer, waved his hand dismissively. "Irrelevant. The will was drafted following the birth of his second son, years before Mr. Archer became ill."

"He would have changed it," Evelyn said acidly, staring at Nora. "If he'd been thinking clearly, he would never have left his children in the care of a cheating, lying b—"

Vince put his hand on Evelyn's arm. "Now, Evvie. There's absolutely no proof that Nora was unfaithful to Harry."

"I am the proof. He told me. He told me she wanted to sleep with Logan Cathcart. And now, with my brother dead less than six months, she *is* sleeping with Logan Cathcart. Is that not proof enough?"

Corrado smiled. "I'm afraid not, Mrs. Gellner. And I think you know that." He turned his placid gaze toward Vince, who was looking flushed, his forehead damp with perspiration.

"And so do you, Mr. Begetti. No judge is going to take these boys away from their mother. Her husband trusted her. The children trust her. We have maybe a hundred character witnesses who will testify to her dedication to Sean and Harry. And you have…?"

Evelyn narrowed her eyes. "I have what I know. I have what my brother told me. I have Logan Cathcart. Make him testify under oath, and then we'll know what really happened. We'll know that she intends to be this man's lover, and God only knows what will become of the boys. She spends all her time over there already. She even drags Sean into it. He's her excuse."

Corrado glanced subtly at Nora. She'd explained everything to him, and he knew that the likelihood of an ongoing relationship with Logan was nearly zero.

Nora hadn't seen or heard from Logan since she left his house last Friday night.

Tomorrow it would be a full week.

The lawyer would like to offer that promise now, to calm the waters. But Nora refused to placate Evelyn with promises that she'd never get involved with Logan again.

Never was a long time. Someday, the horror of Harrison's last months would be a distant memory. Someday, the boys would be older and less vulnerable. Their world would steady, and their confidence would return.

They would be able to trust their mother to love someone else, without thinking it meant she no longer loved them.

And then, who knew what might happen? If Logan were still free...

And still interested in her...

Her heart dragged, well aware what a long shot that was. When would this Eden of peace and freedom finally arrive?

Another six months? A year? Five years?

There was no way Logan would wait that long for her, especially when he'd made it clear the interest was purely physical. The sex had been transforming for her…but a man like him could find a hundred more talented, more desirable lovers in Eastcreek alone.

Women who didn't come with the kind of baggage Nora brought.

But even if she was destined never to touch him again, she wouldn't promise anything that closed the door forever.

Hope was all she had.

The lawyer nodded. They had strategized all this together earlier in the week, as soon as Evelyn had asked for the meeting. They would have to come at her another way.

Nora had put her trust in him. Jim Stilling was a good man, and he said Corrado was the best.

"So," Corrado picked up smoothly. "What your side has is the word of the boys' aunt. A woman who, it might be argued, is hostile toward my client for reasons that have nothing to do with the welfare of the children."

Evelyn sat very erect. "Reasons like what? What are you implying?"

"I'm implying that a ten-thousand-acre ranch is an extremely valuable asset. And that, as Harrison's only sister, you might reasonably have expected to inherit at least some interest in it. And yet, as I recall..."

He shoved around some papers, as if he needed to confirm the facts, which was obviously absurd. He knew full well that Evelyn had inherited nothing. Why should she? She was a rich woman in her own right, having married into a ranch half again as big as Eastcreek.

"Yes, here it is. Apparently your brother left the ranch in its entirety to his widow. My client."

Evelyn's black eyes were sparkling with rage, and red spots appeared on her cheeks. "You think this is about *money?*"

Corrado pulled a dignified, long face, making himself resemble an elegant basset hound. "I'm not sure what it's about, Mrs. Gellner. I find it difficult to believe that a woman of your intelligence really believes she can successfully contest custody of Mrs. Archer's children. Thus, I have to deduce you're after something else. That much money is a fairly powerful incentive."

Evelyn transferred her furious glare to Nora. "This is what you think, as well?"

Nora kept her voice cool. She thought Corrado was on the wrong tack, but he was in charge.

For now.

"I honestly don't know what to think, Evelyn. In your heart, you must know Sean and Harry are safe with me. And yet, you seem willing to put them through the distress of a custody hearing. You want them to see their only two living relatives squabbling over them like dogs over a bone."

Corrado broke in smoothly. "Perhaps we should deal in specifics. It might move things along a little more expeditiously. We're prepared to offer ten thousand cash, and ten acres on the western edge of Bull's Eye Ranch."

Nora's mouth opened. *What?*

But she didn't have time to speak. Evelyn's head snapped back as if the lawyer had slapped her.

"How *dare* you?" Her voice was shaking, with either pain or rage...or both. "Ten thousand dollars? Is it your intention to insult me, Mr. Corrado? That ranch is worth millions."

Nora looked at her hands. She had told the lawyer she'd allow him to follow any strategy he believed would result in Evelyn's surrender, but this was almost too painful to watch.

Evelyn might think Nora didn't deserve to

be mistress of the Archer family ranch, but her objection had nothing to do with greed.

"Very well," Corrado said. "For obvious reasons, Mrs. Archer wants to spare her sons the ordeal of a custody suit. She is prepared to offer fifty thousand dollars, and fifty acres. But this is her final offer."

Nora looked up in time to see Evelyn's eyes narrow.

She tried to speak. A sputtering noise was all that came out.

Then, appalled, Nora witnessed a sight she'd never seen before—and wouldn't have believed was possible.

Tears spilled from Evelyn's hard, black eyes and trailed slowly down her cheeks.

At first, the woman seemed unaware.

"You fool. I don't want my brother's money." Evelyn shook her head, and two more tears fell. "I don't want—" Her voice broke. "A single goddamn cent."

Corrado sighed, resting his hands palms down on the table. "Then perhaps you can tell us what it is you *do* want."

Evelyn made a choking sound, an inelegant noise that seemed to confuse her, as if she couldn't imagine it had come from her mouth.

"I want..." She frowned, and dashed the

tears away with an angry hand. But more fell to replace them, and she didn't seem to be able to control it. "I want…"

"What do you want, Mrs. Gellner?"

She pounded her fists on the table. "I want my brother back!"

The room froze, silence thick in the air. Vince tried to reach out and touch Evelyn's arm, but she jerked away.

She was staring at Nora, shaking her head. "You took him away from me ten years ago. I want those years back. I want his love back."

"Evelyn, no."

"Yes, you did. It was never the same between us, after you came. He knew I didn't trust you, and it drove a wedge between us. From the minute you got there, I was nothing. And now…now you want me to be nothing in his sons' lives, too."

She lowered her face into her hands, her shoulders shaking. Harsh, unnatural noises escaped. She remained that way a minute, then, scraping her chair back violently, she hoisted herself up and left the room.

Vince cleared his throat. "I think perhaps I need to confer with my client, and reschedule—"

Nora stood.

"No. No more meetings."

She moved toward the door, hoping she could catch Evelyn in time.

She found her sister-in-law standing rigidly by the elevator, fumbling in her purse, probably hunting blindly for a tissue. The tears were no longer flowing, but her face was wrecked.

She jabbed the down button, and refused to look at Nora.

"Evvie, please. Listen to me," Nora said. "You're so wrong about Harrison. He always adored you. Always."

Evelyn thrust her shoulders back and her chin out, like a soldier.

"Don't you dare patronize me, Nora. Just don't you dare."

Nora refused to be intimidated. "He idolized you. Didn't you know that? You were his brilliant big sister. You were the best at everything that mattered. He told stories about you, about when you were children together, every day of his life. Your scholarship to school. Your chili that won all the ribbons. How you rode a horse to your senior prom, and how your husband came to him, lovestruck, begging for your hand in marriage."

And there were so many more, hundreds and

hundreds of Evelyn anecdotes. It would take a month to repeat them all.

And suddenly Nora realized that she should have been doing exactly that, in the months since Harrison's death. She'd been so wrapped up in her own grief, her own inadequacies, her own fears for the boys.

She hadn't understood how terrified Evelyn was that, now that Nora didn't have Harrison to answer to, she would shut her unloved sister-in-law out entirely.

"Oh, Evvie." She shook her head. "The ironic thing is that I always knew I couldn't measure up to you. I could never ride like you, or cook, or run a ranch. Harrison loved me, and he loved that I could give him sons, but he didn't really respect me, not the way he respected you. In fact, just before he died, he made me promise to ask you for help, if the ranch became too much for me."

Evelyn shifted her head a quarter turn, just enough to glance at Nora out of the corner of her eye.

"But you don't. You've never asked for my help. Never."

"No," Nora admitted, pushing her pride out of the way for once. "I've been too afraid to

KATHLEEN O'BRIEN   295

admit any weakness. You already thought so little of me."

The elevator chimed softly, and the doors opened. Her time was up.

Evelyn hesitated. She fiddled with her purse.

"I have to go," the older woman said finally.

Nora didn't protest.

She'd said all she could, for now.

"I have to go," Evelyn repeated awkwardly. She looked at Nora. "I have to fix my face. But maybe…maybe we can talk more later."

Nora nodded.

Evelyn got onto the elevator, but at the last minute she put out her hand to prevent the doors from closing.

"You didn't know your lawyer was going to offer me money, did you?"

Nora shook her head. "I did give him carte blanche to see if he could change your mind. But if he'd warned me what he had planned, I could have told him you weren't after money."

"I thought so. Damned *lawyers*." Evelyn raised her brows. "I think I might fire mine. How about you?"

Her expression was poker-faced, but something in her eyes made Nora want to smile.

"Well," she said, pretending to think it over. "Tell you what. I will if you will."

* * *

What a week.

If Logan had thought things would calm down after the open house, he'd been an idiot.

But then, what was new about that?

Calm? If anything, the exact opposite was true. The phone had rung off the hook, with people wanting to schedule demonstrations, or tours, or volunteer to help. And then, right in the thick of it, Vic's wife had decided to go into labor. She'd delivered a ten-pound baby boy on Monday, and Vic had set off on a four-week daddy-leave, effective immediately.

So now Logan was doing his manager's work, too.

Max had already been scheduled for three education demonstrations this week. This one, Friday afternoon at the Eastcreek Elementary School, would be number four.

It was the one Logan felt most ambivalent about. Sean would be one of the kids sitting in the auditorium seats, and that was good. He had something he wanted to talk to him about, if some private time could be managed.

But he also knew that Nora might be there, too.

And he wasn't sure he was ready for that.

As it turned out, he needn't have worried.

Obviously Nora wasn't ready to face him, either. She wasn't anywhere in sight. She was as thoroughly gone as she'd been the night he came back from the sanctuary to find an empty bed.

And a Dear John letter on the pillow.

He'd told himself that night to count his blessings. A vanisher was obviously preferable to a clinger. What if he'd made the mistake of letting Annie Arden into his bed?

At least he didn't have to worry about how to keep Nora from hanging around making him pancakes in the morning.

Yeah. That's what he told himself.

The elementary school show wasn't his best, but luckily the kids were receptive, fairly easy to please.

Even a bird as egotistical as Max could get enough of a good thing, though, and by the end of the demonstration, the old buzzard actually turned his head away from the treats.

But the kids didn't notice, or didn't care. Their applause was thunderous—a hundred kids in an uncarpeted auditorium could definitely make some noise. The Q and A session afterward went on at least five minutes beyond schedule, though Logan didn't let it go to his head. He knew kids would do anything to avoid having to go back to class.

Eventually, the principal made her way onto the stage and invited one more round of applause. Max shrieked his annoyance, which delighted everyone into further clapping.

"How about if one of our students helps you get Max packed up and out to your truck?" The principal, whose name he couldn't remember, was already scanning the auditorium, clearly looking for one of her pet overachievers to reward with the mission.

"Great." He could have kissed her. "How about Sean Archer?"

The woman's eyebrows went up. "Sean?"

"Yeah. He's been helping out at the sanctuary, and he knows the birds. Max can be... funny...with kids he doesn't know."

He cast an apologetic glance at Max, who was busy grooming his feathers and didn't care that he'd been maligned. Max loved everyone, as long as they had a treat in their hand. But the principal didn't need to know that.

"Oh, of course. All right, then." She went up to the microphone and tapped to be sure it was live. "Sean Archer. Sean Archer? Where are you, dear?"

A small commotion at the back signaled

his position. It took a minute, but finally the boy stood, raising his hand. He didn't look as thrilled by the honor as one of the over-achievers might have. He looked surprised, and frankly kind of ticked.

Logan didn't take it personally. Most normal kids—the ones who weren't professional kiss-ups—hated being singled out at school.

But when the principal called, Sean couldn't very well refuse. So he made his way out of his row and up onto the stage.

"Thanks," Logan said with a smile. "You know what to do, right?"

Sean mumbled something back that might have been "you're welcome," but it was hard to tell. He didn't look Logan in the eyes. He just went to work, packing up Max's supplies in the box provided.

As they exited the auditorium, Sean carried the supply box, while Logan hoisted the much heavier Max. They didn't speak at all until they reached the truck and got everything settled.

"Thanks," Logan said again. He looked at Sean's face, trying to judge his emotional state. It felt strange, not seeing him often enough to keep his finger on the pulse. The boy was up and down so often. "How are things going?"

"Okay." Sean cut a quick glance at Logan. "Not great."

"No? How come?"

"I don't know. Mom seems kind of upset."

He scraped at a speck along the door, just above the handle. "I think she might be mad at Aunt Evelyn. She won't let Harry and me go spend the night there tonight. But we always go on Fridays."

Logan was suddenly uncomfortable. He didn't want Sean to talk about Nora. Above all things, he didn't want to stoop to pumping the boy for information about his mother.

Wasn't that exactly what Sean had accused him of?

Besides, he had something else he wanted to tell Sean, before he had to report back for classroom duty.

"I wouldn't worry too much about it," he said. "People fight all the time, and they get over it. Your mom and your aunt will, too."

Sean didn't look convinced, but he didn't openly disagree. He just shrugged and went back to picking at the spot on the door.

"Hey. There's something I wanted to show you." Logan reached into his back pocket and pulled out a piece of sketch paper. He unfolded it and held it out. "What do you think of this idea?"

Sean took the paper reluctantly, as if having a grown-up ask for his opinion made him suspicious.

He squinted down at it in silence for a long minute. Then he looked back up at Logan. "What is this?"

"It's a new area for the sanctuary," Logan said. He bent over and traced his forefinger along the simple diagram. "It's a wildlife trail. It starts over by the pond."

Sean frowned. "But why does the paper say 'Harrison's Pond'?"

"That's what I'm going to call it. Your dad used to take you fishing there a lot, didn't he?"

"A long time ago," Sean said, and Logan's chest tightened, realizing how different a child's frame of reference was.

When he'd first moved here, Logan had been annoyed to see Harrison and his son march out, poles and tackle boxes in hand, to fish in Logan's pond.

When Logan called Harrison on it, the man had explained that Doreen had given them permission. He clearly autocratically assumed that the rights had been granted in perpetuity. And although Logan hadn't been inclined to indulge his arrogant neighbor, he'd taken one look at the excitement in Sean's eyes and decided not to complain.

To Logan, the memory was as clear as yesterday. To the boy, it was already receding. Which meant that someday, all Sean's memories of his father would be as faded and unclear as photos in a dusty scrapbook.

Poor kid. Eight and a half was just plain too young to lose your father.

Sean had gone back to staring at the picture.

"It wasn't both of us," Sean said thoughtfully. "Just me. Harry was too little to fish, and he couldn't ever be quiet. But Dad was really good. He always caught something for dinner, and Milly would cook it." He bit his lower lip. "It was a lot of fun."

"I know. That's why I thought the pond should be named for him."

Logan had never forgotten the poignant moment when Sean had said no one would ever even talk to him about his father anymore.

That it was as if his dad had never existed.

Well, Logan couldn't bring the man back, but he could at least show Sean that his father wasn't forgotten. Maybe, eventually, the boy could still be proud to be Harrison Archer's son.

Sean gave Logan a searching look. "There's

going to be a sign right out there? Where everybody can see it?"

Logan nodded. "Yes. If that's okay with you."

For a minute, Logan thought Sean might actually say no. His brows drew together over his moody hazel eyes, and his lips pinched together.

His fist tightened on the paper. Then he shoved it back into Logan's hand.

"Do whatever you want," he said. "It's your pond."

He took off running toward the front door of the elementary school.

Great. Logan had to laugh at himself. *Nicely done, Mr. Psychiatrist.* That certainly went well.

Leaning against the truck, Logan watched until the goofy red curls had disappeared into the building.

Didn't matter if Sean had pretty much spit his offer back into his face. No way that darn kid was going missing on his watch.

Max let out a screech, clearly tired of being out in the hot spring sun. He tilted his head and grumbled at Logan, sounding exactly like a cantankerous old man.

"I hear you, Max." Logan looked once more

at his sketch, then folded it back up and slid it into his pocket. "And for once I have to agree with you. It is seriously time for me to just give up on that kid."

Chapter Seventeen

Nora had been expecting to feel better, now that relations had calmed down with Evelyn.

They'd all eaten dinner together Friday night. Evelyn had agreed to make her famous chili here at Bull's Eye, though she'd rarely set foot in the kitchen since Nora took over as mistress. Sean and Harry had helped with the cooking, and then had eaten like trenchermen, asking for seconds, then thirds, with a genuine enthusiasm that obviously pleased her.

After dinner, they'd played Monopoly with the boys until their bedtime. Evelyn had left the minute the boys climbed the stairs, obviously not ready for any private time with Nora.

That was okay. After all these years of tension and resentment, it would take a lot longer than one day to reach full détente. For now, Nora was content to enjoy this single glimmer of hope.

But that meant when she woke Saturday feeling headachy, tired and drenched in melancholy, she couldn't lay the blame at her sister-in-law's feet.

The truth was, Evelyn had, in some ways, been a distraction. As long as Nora stayed completely focused on preparing for the custody battle, she'd been able to keep thoughts of Logan at bay.

Now, she had no shield, and here it came... the heartache and regret he'd warned her about.

She had gone to bed aching for his arms, dreamed of him all night and woke up whispering his name.

She pulled the pillow over her head, disgusted with herself. So much for all that warrior bravado. So much for the stoic assurances that one night would be enough, that she could easily handle whatever happened—or didn't happen—between them after.

When tears of self-pity began to burn at the back of her eyes, she jumped out of bed. She would not do this. She would not, under any circumstances, let herself act as wimpy and pathetic as he'd predicted she would.

This was a big house on a big ranch, with big responsibilities. She'd tackle a few of them. She would keep herself so darn busy she didn't have time to think Logan Cathcart's name, much less say it.

The boys wondered what had gotten into her, of course. Saturdays were usually lazy days around Bull's Eye, set aside for Little League games or swim parties or trips downtown for milk shakes and superhero movies.

But today, she worked like a fiend, vacuuming under furniture that hadn't been moved in years, pulling down drapes that needed to go to the cleaners, emptying drawers of clutter accumulated since long before Harry was born.

"Mom, are you okay?"

Sean wandered into the second-floor guest bathroom, dangling his guitar and frowning anxiously at the sight of his mother crouched in the tub, applying caulking to a bare spot along the tiles. "Did Aaron quit or something?"

Aaron was one of the ranch hands who just happened to be a genius with repairs. He'd been doubling as handyman for as long as Nora could remember.

"No," she said. "But he's busy. There's no reason I can't do some of these chores myself."

Sean lingered in the doorway, obviously unsatisfied with that answer.

"I was thinking," he said, a little too casually, "do you want to go over to Two Wings later? Logan did a demonstration at school yesterday, and he said I could come see Hank, as long as I got a grown-up to bring me."

She turned. "Is that how he put it? As long as you got a grown-up to bring you?"

Sean nodded. "Yeah, you know. He meant I couldn't just run off without telling you."

Yes, and he'd also been very careful not to say "get your mother to bring you." He obviously didn't want to encourage that. Well, he needn't worry. She wasn't going to behave like a lovesick teenager, inventing excuses to drive by his house.

"Not today," she said. She didn't look at her son, because she didn't want to see the disappointment on his face. "Today's not a good day. We'll work something out soon, though, I promise."

"All right." Sean started to leave, but at the last minute he turned back. "But you're okay, right, Mom? There's nothing wrong or anything, is there?"

She put feeling into her smile. The last thing she wanted was for him to worry. "Of course not. Everything is fine, honey. Honest."

She must not have been as convincing as she'd hoped, because an hour later, when she went into the great room with a rag and a bottle of leather cleaner, she ran into...

A six-foot, mustached man with Harry's face and Sean's feet, lurching around in one of Harrison's old coats and a Texas Rangers baseball cap.

"She's here!" Harry's stage whisper hissed through the room. Then the "man" wobbled over to the CD player and pushed a button.

Immediately, the sounds of Frank Sinatra, Harrison's favorite, flowed through the room, smooth as oil. He was singing about having too few regrets to mention, because he'd always lived his way.

Nora had always hated that song. But of course, because Harrison loved it, the boys had never heard her say so.

Obviously they believed she needed an emotional lift. This dance at the open house had been their most glorious moment.

And they'd decided to re-create the triumph.

Harry came bobbing toward her, and as he drew close she saw that they'd been far more heavy-handed with the black marker than Logan had been.

The inch-thick mustache dominated his tiny lip, then crawled onto his freckled cheeks, ending in the upturned curlicues ordinarily associated with cartoon villains.

"May I have this dance, Mrs. Archer?" Harry didn't stammer this time. He had obviously perfected his technique with practice.

Nora nodded, smiling. But her heart had begun to ache again, because suddenly Logan was everywhere. The room was full of him. She held her son's small, sticky hands, but this was Logan's dance.

His idea. His gift. She remembered the smile in his eyes as he watched his surrogates twirl her across the amphitheater stage.

When Sinatra's last note died away, she put every ounce of energy she had into her applause.

"Thank you," she said, laughing warmly. And she kissed her boys, one after the other, as she had the night of the open house. "That was a lovely break from my work, kind sir."

But as Sean lifted Harry from his shoulders and let him leap like a frog onto the sofa, she could tell that once again she'd failed. Sean's bewildered frown said that he knew her delight was at least partly feigned.

He just didn't know why.

She would have to do better.

"Hey," she said, affecting excitement, uncomfortably aware that she might be overdoing it a little. "If you guys will help me clean the sofa, maybe we can go to the movies after dinner!"

Harry started to cheer, but when he saw that Sean looked unmoved, his enthusiasm quickly subsided. He always took his cues from his older brother. He didn't want to commit a gaffe that made him appear babyish and uncool.

"If we've got time to go to the movies, we've got time to go to Two Wings." Sean jutted his chin out slightly. "Right?"

Oh, Lord.

"Well, not really," she said, thinking quickly. "Because Two Wings closes at dark. We'll be going to the movies much later than that."

Sean compressed his mouth, rejecting her logic for the specious dodge it was.

"Then no thanks."

He dropped his father's coat onto the sofa and turned away. "I've got some stuff to do myself."

* * *

Several hours later, she decided to try one more time. He might have forgiven her by now. He might be ready to be philosophical.

A movie adventure was better than none at all.

She was even willing to toss in dinner at that terrible pizza place they loved so much. Remembering guiltily that she'd let them eat hot dogs for lunch, she was glad Evelyn wasn't here. She mentally promised herself that she'd feed them nothing but vegetables the whole day tomorrow.

But Sean wasn't in his room.

She wasn't terribly alarmed by that. He'd been so much better the past couple of weeks. She assumed he must have decided to hang out with Harry. He'd been teaching his little brother some guitar chords lately....

Although she would have heard that, surely. Harry's guitar lessons were...memorable.

She opened Harry's door.

"Hey, sweetie," she said. He was playing with his action figures on the floor. "Where's Sean?"

"I don't know," Harry said. He made a crackling noise, like a million pieces of glass breaking, then swept his hand through a line of plastic monsters, knocking them over with a string of ever more grisly sound effects.

Maybe downstairs, then.

Maybe in the kitchen with Milly.

Nora started to back away when Harry lifted his head suddenly.

"Oh!" He made his "oops" face. "Mom, wait! I forgot!"

"What?"

Harry dropped his superhero and clambered up to his feet. He ran over to his nightstand and grabbed a piece of paper that had been lying there.

"Sean said to give you this."

Something hitched in her chest. *Oh, God,* she thought. *Not again...*

"Are you mad because I didn't tell you he was leaving?" Harry held out the paper bravely, but his expression was wary. "He said it's just a game. He promised he wasn't being bad again."

"It's okay, honey," she said. She took the paper and read what Sean had written there.

ALL ABOUT SEAN, he'd put in full capitals across the top.

Then, below that, *How well do you know me? If you know where my favorite tree is, that's where you'll find your next clue.*

So was it some kind of test? Was he putting her love on trial?

If she could answer the questions right, she could find him?

And if she couldn't?

But this wasn't a test she could ever in her life fail—these two boys had been her whole life for the past decade. She knew more about Sean Robert Archer than he knew about himself.

"Harry, come with me, honey. I want you to help Milly in the kitchen while I play Sean's game."

"Can't I come?" Harry looked crestfallen. "I like games."

"Next time, maybe," she said. "But right now Milly needs your help."

"Okay."

She tousled his curls affectionately, grateful for at least one child who could resign himself comfortably to any decision.

It took Nora only about two seconds to give Milly a general idea of what was happening.

"That is one high-maintenance boy," the housekeeper muttered under her breath, as she glanced at Sean's "game."

Then she turned to Harry, smiling broadly.

"Come on, sunshine! I've been wondering who was going to lick this bowl for me."

She went outside, thinking about the first clue.

Sean's favorite tree.

That didn't even require thinking. Harrison had built the boys an elaborate fort in the arms of a hundred-year-old oak, and the three of them had slept up there in comfort many a night.

After Harrison got sick, Sean climbed up into the fort whenever he wanted to be alone.

It was just on the other side of the foreman's building. Nora walked, hoping she might see Sean along the way. But she saw only the normal, bustling life of the ranch.

It was only about four in the afternoon, still piercingly hot. She gathered her hair in the back, then looped it around itself in a makeshift ponytail. It probably looked dreadful, but she had to get the thick curls off her neck.

She wished she'd taken a minute to change into sneakers, too. She'd been housecleaning in sandals, which didn't handle the sand and pebbles very well.

But the tree wasn't far.

As she neared, she was relieved to see a small brown paper bag lying in a nook of one of the large, twisting roots. She wasn't crazy about heights, and though she would have climbed up to the fort if she had to, she wouldn't have enjoyed it.

The bag held Sean's MP3 player, and another note.

It was an anagram. She had to smile. Either this wasn't a real test, or Sean must not have much faith in her puzzle-solving skills, because he'd given her a hint, too.

The first song I learned on my guitar, was the hint.

She laughed, not needing even to look at the anagram. She'd heard that song at least a million times.

"The Yellow Rose of Texas."

Another easy clue. At the western edge of the property, right where it abutted the eastern edge of Two Wings, wild yellow roses grew in profusion, climbing an old, sagging fence.

The roses were called Harrison's Yellow, and had nothing to do with the Archers, but the boys refused to believe the beautiful flowers hadn't been named for their daddy.

Harrison wasn't sentimental about sharing a name. Every time they passed the area, Harrison would click his tongue and say, "I've got to get Aaron to take that damn fence down," and Nora would protest, petitioning for the life of the roses.

The walk to the fence was a little longer. Her feet were dusty beyond saving now, though, so it didn't much matter. Whatever small part of her had been worried about Sean relaxed, and she decided to enjoy the game.

Sure enough, beside the yellow roses lay another little brown paper bag. In this one, she found a small box of chocolates and yet another note.

She looked at the chocolates. None of them had melted much. They hadn't been here long.

She glanced around her, in case Sean was still nearby, but nothing moved except the leaves of the overhanging elm. They blew the scent of the roses everywhere.

No other sign of activity. She heard a lawnmower purring in the distance, but this side of the property wasn't the business end. All the stables and barns were east of the hacienda.

Finally, she gave up and looked at the note.

If you remember what my favorite card game was when I was a kid, you'll know where to go next.

When he was a kid…

She found that line bittersweet. All children believed they were more grown-up than they really were. But for Sean, the days before his father's illness probably did seem like a glorious Eden from a far distant past.

So, what had he loved, back "when he was a kid?"

She remembered quickly. He'd been obsessed with Go Fish. For months, he'd insisted on card games instead of bedtime stories.

Go Fish.

Oh…of course. The little blue pond.

Harrison had often taken Sean there to fish, even though it didn't belong to them. With his first son, he'd fished at Green Fern Pond, but after Paul died Harrison refused to go back there…until that terrible day.

Instead, the little blue pond had become the new fishing hole. The pond wasn't even on their property, but somehow Harrison had coaxed Doreen…

And, just like that, light dawned.

The pond was a few yards over the property line dividing Bull's Eye from Two Wings.

The pond belonged to Logan.

She couldn't decide whether to laugh, or to be seriously annoyed.

Sean had been hell-bent on visiting Two Wings today, and, with this silly, serpentine treasure hunt, he'd managed to lead her right where he wanted her.

No wonder the clues had been so easy.

When she found the little scoundrel, she'd let him know exactly what she thought of this...

But she did want to find him.

She picked her way through the overgrown path. Now that Harrison was gone, the brambles had begun to reclaim their own.

The Archers didn't come to the pond anymore.

Nora didn't fish, just as she didn't do any of the other things a traditional Texas rancher's wife should do.

"I'm sorry, Harrison," she said impulsively. She felt close to him, out here on the land he'd loved so much. And she felt that he understood, perhaps, how glad she'd be, someday, to turn this ranch over to the boys.

Maybe, from the broader, wiser perspective of the afterlife, he even understood about Logan.

The rail separating the two ranches was low and easy to step over. After another two or three minutes, she was within sight of the pond. It was a beautiful body of water, small but perfect, fed from Clayton's Creek, bowing out in a perfect oval among the wildflowers and the pines.

She wondered if Sean would be here, or whether there would be still another clue.

Something about an owl, probably. She had no doubt that her stubborn son was going to lead her right to that clinic door, one way or another.

"Nora."

She came around the wide, rough trunk of a poplar, and there he was.

Not Sean, but Logan.

She stopped in her tracks, dismayed.

She cringed at the thought of how scruffy and unkempt she must look, after hours of housework, and then all this tramping around in the dust and heat.

But that prick to her vanity was nothing compared to the misery of realizing that, in spite of her superhuman efforts to avoid pining and obsessing, and hungering for a glimpse of anything that belonged to him, it would now undoubtedly look as if she'd been doing exactly that.

"Logan. I—" Oh, how to explain anything as silly and tortured as Sean's trail of brown paper bags? "Sean...he created this crazy game—"

"I know." Logan's smile was oddly bemused. She realized abruptly that he didn't seem one bit surprised to see her.

She paused, looking at him carefully for the first time.

He, too, was holding a little brown bag.

And half a dozen yellow climbing roses.

"Oh, no," she breathed. "He didn't…"

"Yeah." Logan extended the roses to her. "I think he did."

It didn't make any sense, but instinct took over. She accepted the roses, which smelled as sweet as ever, though they'd wilted slightly in the heat.

"Thank you," she said awkwardly.

He smiled. "And I see you have something for me."

"What?" She looked down. "Oh. The chocolates?"

"My favorites. How did you know?"

She flushed, but then she saw that his eyes were twinkling. He was kidding.

"I didn't know, of course," she said. "But apparently Sean did."

"He's a very observant kid," he said, still smiling. "You've got to give him that."

She laughed. "Oh, I'll give him something, all right, when I finally find him."

Logan tilted his head. "I'm afraid that might not be for a while. You see, he seems to have arranged it so that I'd get here first, and he left me a whole sheet of instructions."

She felt stupid, because this wasn't making much sense.

"Instructions about what? Please, don't let it be another string of clues. If it is, I'm calling the police, and they can put that slippery little eel in a jail cell, for all I care, because he—"

"Nora." Logan cleared his throat. "Let's see what he says. Okay. First, I'm supposed to tell you that Sean is okay. He's back at home with Harry, playing video games. Milly is going to order them pizza for dinner, so there's, and I quote, absolutely nothing to worry about."

"What?" She couldn't make up her mind whether to laugh or strangle her son. "If Sean is back at home with Harry, then what is all this—"

"That brings me to the next item, I think." Logan consulted his list. "No, the second thing is to give you the flowers. I already did that."

He took a step closer. "But now you have to give me the chocolates."

It was like being inside a fun house. Nothing made sense, and she wondered if she should just stop trying to make it do so.

She extended the box numbly.

"Okay. And then," he said, reading carefully. "Then I'm supposed to dance with you. He put some of your favorite songs on the MP3 player. He says you have it. Do you?"

She looked down at the little bag. "Yes."

"Good. We'll have to share the earphones, he says, but he says to tell you it's okay, because he did wash them first."

She laughed, in spite of herself. She'd nagged him so many times about that.

"Logan—" She shook her head helplessly. "I have no idea what Sean thinks he's up to."

"Well, it seems to me he's actually been pretty clever. Clearly he wants to make sure we stop dithering around and finally say some of the things we need to say."

She couldn't tell exactly what he meant. His face was so mock-serious, as if he were dedicated to carrying out Sean's instructions to the letter.

"I'm sorry he's dragged you into this game," she said. "I refused to bring him over here today, and he wanted to come so badly. I think he was just—"

"Why wouldn't you bring him?"

"Because..." She decided just to say it. "Because I didn't want to…to cling. I wanted to give you space."

"You'd already given me a whole week." He raised one eyebrow. "That's space enough for a man to go mad in."

"But—" She gazed at him, afraid to read too much into anything he said. "Logan, I—"

"Wait," Logan said firmly, waving Sean's letter toward her with that pretend-earnest attitude. "There's one more instruction. And it's the most vitally important one of all."

She waited. She felt the butterflies trying to lift her off the ground, but at the same time she was so afraid.

What if he didn't mean what she thought he meant?

"Okay. Apparently I have to tell you I love you."

She stopped breathing.

"Yeah, I've got to." He shrugged. "I was hoping to wait until we were alone together, preferably in bed, but I can't disobey a direct order, right?"

"Logan…you don't have to—"

"Well, it says right here." Logan looked up, grinning. "Yes, I'm afraid I absolutely have to."

Had Sean really…?

She grabbed the paper from his hand.

"It says nothing of the sort," she said, laughing. She handed him back the list. "So I guess you're off the hook. I'm happy to have the roses, but you don't have to say a single word about love."

"Oh, yes, ma'am, I do." With a low growl, Logan pulled Nora into his arms. "I have to say a great many words, in fact. I've spent too long holding it in, and now I'm not sure I can shut up about it."

He kissed the side of her mouth. "I'll start with love." He kissed the other side. "And joy."

She had begun to smile. She was suddenly aglow with happiness. She wondered if she'd ever stop smiling...

"And love again." He drew back, and looked deep into her eyes. "I love you, Nora. I've loved you since the day I met you, when I had no right even to think about you."

She touched his face. She didn't speak, because she was terrified of stopping this glorious flow of words. This, from a man who never spoke of feelings...

"And I need you, Nora. I need you desperately. In my bed, in my life, in my heart."

She realized that she was holding her breath, but she couldn't remember how to start breathing again. Happiness had expanded like a bubble and it took up all the room in her chest.

"Sean has clearly given us his blessing, Nora. Now it's up to you."

At that moment, her cell phone, snugged deep in the pocket of her shorts, chirped.

The sound of an incoming text message.

He smiled, aware that no declaration of love, no proposal of marriage, would be more important than hearing from her boys.

She pulled the phone free and, tilting her head, tried to read it in the bright afternoon sunlight.

It was from Sean.

is he there? did he kiss u?

She held it out so that Logan could see.

"What a little devil." He took the phone and typed in his own text. He offered it to Nora, to get her approval.

I want to, but I think she's worried about you. You okay with me kissing her? And maybe even being her boyfriend? Like all the time?

He smiled. "Send?"

She looked into his sexy eyes. She saw the kindness there, the understanding that nothing, not even this crazy, newfound passion, could make her do anything that might harm her boys. She even saw something nurturing in those eyes, as if he, too, felt the need to protect Sean and Harry.

And then she nodded. "Send."

The several seconds it took to get a response seemed to last forever.

Finally, the phone chirped again.

Heck, yeah, I'm ok with that!

Logan smiled at Nora. "Well?"

His voice didn't sound as if it belonged to him. She realized suddenly that he hadn't been breathing normally, either.

"What's your answer, Nora? Will you let me be a part of your life? Of their lives, too?"

Somehow, she managed to keep her face sober and thoughtful, as pseudo-serious as his had been before. She glanced one more time at her son's text. *Heck, yeah...*

She slipped the cell phone into her pocket.

"Nora..." Logan reached out and pulled her in. "Answer me! I can't wait much longer. I've

waited a hundred years already, just in the past seven days."

She gazed into his intense blue eyes, trying to see the future. He would not be an easy lover. He had grown used to being alone. He found it difficult to share his emotions. The tragedy from his past would always haunt him.

Evelyn would always be suspicious of him, and she'd be a burr under their saddle, probably for the rest of their lives. All of Eastcreek would gossip, at least a little.

And then, she had her own personal fears and insecurities to overcome.

He was younger than she was…and so beautiful. He could have anyone.

Would he regret this moment someday, when he faced the reality of taking on a needy widow and two feisty boys with abandonment issues?

His lips were so close to hers she could feel the warm mint of his breath. His hands pulled her in, with the same gentle mastery she'd seen him use so often on the wounded birds.

"Nora. Don't torture me. Give me your answer."

She took one last deep breath. She lifted her chin.

"My answer is…"

His arms tightened around her, and she smiled.

"Heck, yeah."

Chapter Eighteen

Six months later

The November sunshine was fading, but the brick courtyard of the hacienda, which had absorbed the heat, was still pleasantly warm. Looking for privacy, Logan, Sean and Harry each grabbed a lounger and spread out so they could talk over Logan's dilemma comfortably.

Evelyn was inside, cooking dinner as this was Milly's night off. Nora would be home from her faculty by five o'clock—she'd taken a teaching job this fall.

They had maybe another half an hour alone, so they had to stay focused.

"I didn't know you had any *choice* about how to ask a girl to marry you," Sean said, shrugging as he popped his last piece of contraband taffy into his mouth. "I thought there was like a rule, you know, that you had to kneel down and get all sappy and hold out a ring and kiss her feet or something."

Harry frowned. "Gross. Kiss Mom's *feet?*"

Sean brushed his little brother aside irritably. "Or maybe her hand. I don't know. Do I look like I've asked anybody to marry me lately?"

Harry turned to Logan, bright-eyed. "Maybe you should buy her a puppy from Aunt Evelyn. Mom really wants a puppy, so that would probably make her say yes."

Logan and Sean exchanged a knowing smile. It was an open secret that Harry was dying to get one of Ginger's new litter when they were weaned.

"That's a pretty good idea," Logan said. "And of course I'm definitely going to do the knee thing. Anything else occur to you guys? I want to get this right. Think how embarrassing it would be if she said no."

Sean laughed. "Yeah, right. Like she'd ever say no. I wish you could have seen her while you were gone. Whenever the phone rang, she nearly fell down trying to get to it. And then she'd be all goofy and smiling when she hung up, and she'd laugh for no reason. It was like talking to you made her dumb."

Logan felt a pretty stupid smile creeping across his own face. He was mighty glad to hear that. The two weeks he'd spent in Maine had seemed like an eternity. The last few days, he'd been such a mess he started dreaming that Denver Lynch was dating Nora, and that Logan had come home to find her engaged to the vet.

But, hard as it had been to leave her, he'd needed to make the trip.

He had to be sure he was ready. This marriage was the biggest, scariest step he'd ever contemplated taking. He'd been a terrible husband the first time around. Had he grown up enough to make this time any better?

Would he know how to make Nora happy? Not just in bed, not just in the honeymoon haze of passion, but for the long haul, in sickness and in health, in tragedy as well as in joy?

And, scary as being a husband sounded, it was a walk in the park compared to fatherhood.

Was he ready to provide what Sean and

Harry needed? Was he free to love them without reservation?

He couldn't ask to be their father if his heart was still buried with the son he'd lost.

Nora and the boys had suffered because of that kind of half-love before. He wouldn't put them through it again.

So he'd traveled to Maine to make peace with his past. He'd stayed with his parents, but he'd spent hours, days, with Ben and Rebecca and Chloe, just talking.

Facing the years of repressed feelings with honesty, and speaking them out loud.

Finally.

He was there for Chloe's second birthday. After the party, the four of them had made a pilgrimage to the cemetery to put flowers on Danny's grave. Logan had been so afraid of that moment. He'd been terrified that he wouldn't be able to hold it together, that he might fall apart...

And he did. God help him, he did. He went entirely to pieces, on his knees, right there in front of all of them. But to his surprise, it didn't feel crazy, or weak. It felt long overdue.

No one tried to stop him. In fact, Rebecca had turned her face into Ben's chest, and her shoulders were shaking, too.

Chloe, who still wore her birthday crown made of bits of ribbon from her packages, watched Logan silently for a long time. And then, she had come up and kissed his cheek.

It was hard to explain the effect that gesture of innocent affection had on him. It had been as sweet, as healing, as if it had been Danny's kiss, transmitted through his little half sister's lips.

And, somehow, on the way home, Logan found himself telling her stories about Danny. About the time Rebecca thought Danny had swallowed a lizard and left incoherent, panicked messages with Logan's secretary. About the day Danny ate five bananas and then would never eat a banana again. About the night he coaxed a chipmunk in through his bedroom window and named him Frankie Furball.

Once, he'd even found himself laughing. At that moment, Rebecca had reached out, and he had taken her hand without hesitation. They had laughed together, remembering the good times.

And he knew, finally, that he was ready.

The next day, Ben went with him to the jewelry store, to pick out the ring. Logan spent too much, though he knew price didn't matter to Nora. She didn't care that she had a lot of money, and he didn't. They'd talked about all this, as they had about so many things, over the past six months.

In her eyes, she'd said, the Archer money wasn't hers, anyhow. Though Harrison had attached no strings, trusting her utterly, Nora had always believed she was merely the guardian for the boys.

But Logan wanted the ring to be worthy of her, so he bought a blue sapphire with a clear, rainbowed diamond on either side. He thought she'd like it. And besides, it reminded him of her, the deep, peaceful strength of her love placed protectively between her two sons.

He pulled it out now and opened the blue velvet box. He extended it toward Sean and Harry. "What do you think?"

The boys jumped out of their loungers and came over to get a closer look. They made the appropriate oohs and aahs, though they probably would have liked a rhinestone gumball prize just as well.

"So, where are you going to do it?" Sean glanced around, chewing on his lip thoughtfully. "Out here?"

"I don't know," Logan said. "That was what I was hoping you guys could help me with. Can you think of anywhere really romantic?"

"How about in the tree house?"

"Maybe at a fancy restaurant?"

"I know—" Sean held up his hands excitedly. "How about by the owl house, in the dark? You could—"

A sudden noise sounded in the archway that led to the living room. Logan looked up to find Evelyn standing there, her oven mitt in her hand. She had clearly been watching them, her face expressionless and her body language guarded.

Both boys tensed, as if they thought they might get in trouble. Sean scooped his taffy papers into his palm and squeezed hard, making so much rustle he practically guaranteed he'd get caught spoiling his dinner.

Even Logan had to resist an urge to flip the velvet box shut and tuck it behind his back. Instead, he smiled politely and waited. He knew Evelyn had heard what they were talking about.

If she had something to say, she might as well get it off her chest.

For a long moment, she looked from one of them to the other slowly. No one made a peep. Logan thought Harry might be holding his breath.

As they waited, Evelyn slapped the oven

mitt into the palm of her hand a couple of times, rhythmically. The moment hung heavy, fraught with unspoken implications.

Then, acting on instinct, he held out the box.

"I bought this for Nora," he said. "Do you think she'll like it?"

Evelyn hesitated. Then she gazed into the box, still poker-faced, and studied the ring.

"Very nice," she said stiffly.

"Thanks." He continued to wait. One way or another, he knew she wasn't finished. She and Nora had made great strides in their relationship over the past months, but Logan had tried not to intrude on that. He had no idea how she really felt about the idea of a new husband for Nora, a new father for the boys.

"Logan, I—" Evelyn stopped. She squared her shoulders, took a deep breath and moved out into the courtyard.

"I don't know if you knew this, but my father proposed to my mother out by the fountain in front of the house." She wandered a few feet away, picking dead leaves from the creeper that covered the south courtyard wall, obviously not quite ready to meet his eyes.

"Did he?"

"Yes. At midnight. It's lovely in the dark. It's quite romantic, really, with the fountain murmuring, and the stars like silver glitter overhead. And you know the fountain has colored lights that..."

She seemed to realize she was wandering off point. "Anyhow, later, Douglas took me there when he was ready to propose. So you might say it's something of an Archer family tradition."

Logan hesitated, treading carefully. "But..."

She turned finally, and met his gaze straight on. "But what?"

"But Nora isn't an Archer."

Harry sat up straight, clearly shocked. "Of course she is," he insisted indignantly.

Logan looked at Evelyn.

And finally, she smiled.

"Of course she is," she echoed. "She'll always be an Archer, even when she's also a Cathcart."

Logan stood, and without asking permission he walked over and wrapped his arms around the older woman. She bristled, but after a couple of seconds she unbent at least a millimeter.

She actually patted his back, murmuring, "Well, well. That's all right, then."

And then she pulled back, looking uncomfortable as hell.

But Logan felt like singing.

"Hey, guys! What's going on here? Oh—Logan!"

Suddenly, her keys still in her hand, Nora came flying out to the courtyard, her face aglow with smiles. "Logan, I didn't know you were already home!"

He swept her into his arms, his heart soaring, and swung her around, just from the sheer joy of seeing her again. He had so much to tell her. The proposal, the ring…all that was only part of it. The ring just was his way of guaranteeing he had their whole lifetime to talk, and laugh, and love.

"I came early," he said, kissing her neck. "I missed you too much."

Harry grabbed on to his mother's waist, eager to be part of the group hug.

"Logan bought you a ring, Mom," the boy babbled happily, "and it's real, and he said a puppy is really romantic, and he's going to take you to the fountain because you are, too, an Archer, but Aunt Evelyn isn't mad, so it's okay, and—"

Sean growled at his brother. "Harry, you are such a loser! Haven't you ever heard of a secret?"

"Enough!" Evelyn cleared her throat loudly. "I expect two helpers in the kitchen right this minute. In this household, any little boys who want to eat taco casserole had better be willing to cook it."

"But—"

"Kitchen," she said firmly, and though she'd mellowed over these past months she still could trot out the tone that brooked no opposition. "Immediately."

Sean dragged his reluctant brother into the house, following in their aunt's authoritative wake. Once they cleared the courtyard, there was much giggling, and whispering, and fussing back and forth.

Nora looked at Logan, a question in her eyes. "And what, exactly, was that all about, Mr. Cathcart?"

"I can't tell you," he said. "Not till midnight."

"Pretend it's midnight now."

He looked at her, and he knew she knew. Her eyes were sparkling, and her lips were soft and ready....

"Okay," he said. He pulled her close, her back against his chest. He ran his forefingers over her eyes, smoothing her eyelids shut. "But we have to do it right. We're outside. It's midnight. It's chilly and clear, and the night is full of silver stars."

She leaned her head back against his shoulder. She murmured, a small, purring, blissful sound. "Okay. I like that. You look very sexy by starlight."

"So do you." He ducked his head and kissed her neck, then her collarbone, her ear, her hair.... It was all he could do to stop.

"Okay. Now pretend we're out front, beside the fountain."

"Why the—"

"Shh." He wrapped his arms tighter across her rib cage, just under the warm swell of her breast. "We're beside the fountain. It's whispering to us. It splashes in the starlight. Now and then, little drops of water land on our faces."

"And you kiss them away."

He felt his groin tighten. "Yes," he said. "I kiss them away, because I don't want you to be cold."

She tilted her head back, trying to smile up at him. "And because you *want* to kiss me."

"Yes." His voice had deepened, as he realized once more how much he loved this woman, how desperately he wanted to protect her, and bring her the happiness she deserved. He said a quick prayer that he would be able to do those things, in spite of the fact that he wasn't nearly good enough for her. "Yes, I always, always want to kiss you."

"Good." She took a deep, satisfied breath. "And then?"

"And then… I give you this."

Though he was reluctant to let go of her, he found the jewelry box and opened it.

"I give you this ring, and I ask you if you'll do me the honor of being my wife."

For a frozen second she was completely still. And then, slowly, she turned in his arms. "Logan," she said, staring at the ring. "It's… it's beautiful. But, Logan, are you sure?"

"Sure that I want to be married to you? That I want to spend the rest of my life with you and the boys? Yes. As sure as I am that I want my heart to keep beating."

"But we—" She hesitated, glancing toward the living room, as if she feared Sean and Harry might be listening. "We are a complicated package. It won't be…easy."

He smiled. "Maybe not. But it will be a heck of a lot easier than trying to live without you. That's something I could never do."

She opened her mouth, but shut it again almost immediately. Her eyes clouded over, and he sensed that she was troubled.

What was wrong? It wasn't that she didn't

love him. She'd proved that, over and over. And she wanted to say yes. He could feel the yearning inside her, because it echoed the same hungry longing that pulsed inside of him.

But something was holding her back.

"What is it, sweetheart?" He pulled her close again, this time facing him so that he could search her eyes. "You love me, I know it. Is there some reason you're afraid to say yes? I promise you, I'll work hard to deserve you. If you're ever unhappy a day in your life, my love, it won't be because of me."

"I know." She touched his face. "It's just that... You see... I would like another child, Logan. Someday. Your child."

He almost laughed, from sheer relief. Of course...that was her fear. He should have known. He should have talked about this first. He should have told her that he'd brought no ghosts home with him from Maine. Only memories, bittersweet but beautiful memories of his first son.

But he'd been in such a hurry...

He smiled, washed through with happiness. The past couldn't come between them. Not anymore.

He kissed the side of her mouth. "Just one child?"

"Just one…?" She frowned, as if she weren't sure she'd heard him correctly.

"You want only one more child?" He brushed back her curls and kissed the pulse at the edge of her temple. "I was thinking maybe two, at least. Two girls, perhaps. To keep Sean and Harry from getting too big for their britches."

Her fingers tightened on his arms. Her smile was tremulous still, but it held the promise of a brilliant intensity, like the sun struggling out of the clouds.

"Logan, have you thought—"

"I've thought of nothing else, Nora. Nothing but you and Sean and Harry, and the crazy, wonderful family we can make together. I love you. I love Sean and Harry. Please. Say you'll marry me, and let's get started."

"Logan, I—"

With a stampede of feet, Harry suddenly appeared in the doorway. Sean was right behind him, grabbing at his arm.

"Mom," Harry said plaintively, his face woebegone in the shadows as he struggled to resist his big brother's efforts to pull him away. "Please, Mom. Tell Logan yes."

She smiled at her son. "Is that what you want, honey? Do you want me to say yes?"

"I do!" Harry wrestled his arm away from Sean's.

"Harry, come on—"

"I really, really do, Mom," Harry insisted. "Because Aunt Evelyn says we can't eat her taco casserole till you and Logan are done. And I'm starving."

Sean groaned with disgust. "You moron! This isn't about food!"

"Well, that's easy for you to say," Harry whined, his voice receding as Sean finally managed to haul him back into the house. "You had about a million taffies, so you're not even..."

The sounds faded away. Logan and Nora exchanged looks, and then, simultaneously, they burst into helpless laughter.

"I told you," she said, wiping the moisture of mirth from her eyes. "It's not going to be easy. It's going to be positively insane."

"Maybe so." He held out the ring, a question in his eyes. "But your starving son and I beg you, Nora. Say yes."

Shaking her head and laughing softly still, she extended her hand.

As he slipped the sapphire and diamonds onto her fragile finger, he felt that it was trembling. His fingers might have been shaking, too, a little.

"My love," he whispered. "My wife."

"Yes," she answered, finally saying the word he'd waited so long to hear. "With all my heart, yes."

* * * * *